Box
Ken vas had
now become something of an obsession. It was the first time he had been really stretched since he had left the Brigade and there was only the odd incident of the gasometer to remind him that Box 13 would ever produce anything of interest . . .

He had not gone far on his motor bike when he passed a mangled Cortina being extricated from a lamp post by a breakdown crew. He slowed down to scrutinise it closely but the wreck offered no clue. Then he approached the first of the Brandons he had looked up in the directory – a greengrocer's shop. Ken parked the bike, dismounted and went thoughtfully in.

Boon

ANTHONY MASTERS

Based on the Central television series created by
Jim Hill and Bill Stair

SPHERE BOOKS LIMITED
London and Sydney

First published in Great Britain by
Sphere Books Ltd, 1986
30–32 Gray's Inn Road, London WC1X 8JL

Based on the television series BOON produced by Central
Independent Television plc

TRADE
MARK

Set in 10 on 12pt Linotron Century Schoolbook

Printed and bound in Great Britain by
Collins, Glasgow

Chapter One

Harry stood in the bathroom, trying to work out what he was going to say. Right now, Spain seemed a million miles away, and however successful he was going to be, however much Alison had set her heart on their escape route – he was still going to miss White Watch like crazy. The easy companionship, the continuous teasing, the ready laughter, the action, the danger, the teamsmanship – he was going to miss all that. Badly. It hurt now, so God knows what it was going to be like in Spain. He'd never stop thinking about them.

Of course she'd had a tough job to persuade him – she knew that. They all knew that. Time after time she had returned to the attack, probing, worrying at his future. Or, as she said, the lack of it. Now the familiar conversation re-ran in his mind, and he heard the echo of Alison's strident voice.

'You've no future.'

'So you say.'

'You'll be invalided out.'

'Thanks.'

'And if not that – there's only that lousy little pension.'

'It's not bad.'

'It's terrible.'

'Look, love. Can you imagine me behind a bar in Spain?'

'I can imagine you behind a bar anywhere,' she insisted. 'Come on, Harry. Be ambitious for a change. Think of *us*.'

'I am.'

'I know.' Her voice took on a note of grating sarcasm. 'It's a nice, safe job.'

'It is!'

'And what do I get out of it?' Her voice was shrill. 'Rotting away in a semi like this. Nowhere to go, nothing to do.'

'You've got the—'

'Townswomen's Guild. Thanks.'

'And the shop.'

'Let me assure you, helping out in a grocers is just what I've always wanted. I mean – it's all go. Much more of a rave up than the Costa Brava.'

'Alison—'

'It's no good, Harry.' She sounded even harsher now. 'If you won't do it, I will.'

'Who with?'

'I'll find someone. Or do it on my own if necessary. I'm not a complete cabbage.'

'Like me.'

'You said it.'

And so the conversations had drummed on until, one day, he had weakened. It had been a particularly dull week and hour after monotonous hour had been spent in the rest room, sipping weak tea and eating biscuits. Somehow, Alison had sensed his vulnerability and gone straight for the jugular.

'So it's either Spain and me – or me in Spain.'

'Oh yeah?'

'I'm going. You've got the choice. The Costa Brava – or English weather.'

The week had also consisted of grey skies and drizzling rain. Suddenly Harry wondered what it might be like.

'Well—'

She saw his indecision and went in harder. 'It'll be lovely. Lovely. Just the two of us.'

'S'pose we go bust?'

'On the Costa Brava? With a bar?' She had looked at him incredulously. 'You're barmy.'

Maybe he was.

'We'll be making our fortunes.'

'I'm not cut out for the sun.'

'You'll be bronzed.'

'Red and peeling.'

But she knew he was weakening and she grabbed his arm. 'Darling – it'll be a fresh start.'

'Eh?'

'Our marriage – it's stale. It'll blossom in the sun.'

'Mm.'

'You see the prices. The facts and figures. Give it a swing, Harry.'

'All right.'

'What?' Despite everything she looked astounded.

'I said all right. We'll go.'

'You mean it?'

'I mean it.'

She had flung her arms round his neck. 'You lovely, lovely man. You're the tops.'

Chapter Two

White Watch were assembled in the fire station's stuffy recreation room. It was a very male room, with pin-up posters on the wall and a pile of dirty cups in the sink. But tonight there was an air of expectancy.

'Splashing on the Brut, is he?' asked Roger.

'Come on, Harry,' yelled Ken. 'Stop tartin' yourself up.'

'Think he's got the message?' asked Pete.

'He shouldn't have,' snapped Roger. 'It's meant to be a bleedin' surprise, innit? – I mean, it's not every day a bloke leaves the brigade.'

'Do you reckon he thinks we've forgotten all about it?'

'Dunno what he thinks. Harry!' Ken yelled upstairs again, rather more impatiently.

'Don't let him ramble on all night,' said Pete cynically.

'He's got about fifty pages.' Ken sounded depressed. 'He's probably out there learning it.'

'You watch, though. He'll deny all knowledge,' said John.

'Where's his present?' Roger handed Ken an untidy package. 'What the hell's this? I thought we were giving him a teasmade.'

'We are. This is to pour into his tankard. Suntan lotion.'

'*Olé*!' sang out Pete.

'I'm going to miss the miserable bugger,' put in Ken reflectively, but Roger disagreed.

'I'm not. Jammy sod!'

'Well I love him,' Ken told the room just as Harry entered with a quiet dignity, faking innocence of the impending celebrations. His colleagues did the same.

'Was somebody shouting for me?' Harry asked.

'No,' replied Ken stolidly.

'Just thought I heard a bit of a racket.'

There was no response.

'What's happening then?' Harry asked a little wearily. He was suddenly tired of the game. He looked around at their fake puzzled expressions.

'What do you mean? Like a fire or something?' Ken's sally was greeted with tepid laughter.

'You winding me up?'

'No.'

'He smells nice,' Pete told everybody. Then he confided, 'You smell nice, Harry.'

'It's my last night. I just thought I'd . . .'

'Is it?' John's innocence verged on the absurd.

'It's not, is it, Harry? Tomorrow, surely.'

'No. Tonight. You're all winding me up, you bastards.'

'We're not, mate.'

Suddenly Harry was disappointed. Surely they weren't going to do nothing. Nothing at all? He tried to cope. 'Well, I'm off anyway. I even had a few words prepared. Just to say thank you to all you lads on White Watch, and well nothing really. I had it written down . . . It's been over twenty years, you know.' He paused.

'Sorry, Harry. We all thought it was tomorrow.' Ken adopted a tone of injured innocence.

'Do you want a drink or something, Harry, just for a sort of goodbye toast?' asked John.

But Harry was now set into his martyrdom. 'No matter. I don't like a lot of fuss.'

'That's what I thought. He doesn't like a lot of fuss.' John sounded full of depressing common sense.

Ken, savouring the moment, kept up the act. 'I feel really choked about this. We've let you down, mate.' He turned to the others. 'Haven't we? Anybody got some beer in?'

'Anybody got anything?' repeated John.

'I have got a drop – coke or something. Will that do?'

Then, to Harry's bewilderment, all the members of White Watch softly began to sing the first few bars of 'Viva España'. 'Da dee da dee da dee da da, che viva España!' They ended on a rising crescendo whilst Ken, who had surreptitiously whipped out a bottle of bubbly from the fridge, began to shake it with great enthusiasm. As he opened it he pointed the top towards Harry.

'I'm bloody soaked,' he commented, wiping the foam out of his eyes whilst the others chanted, 'Che viva España!'

There was an outburst of back-slapping, polaroids and good humour whilst Harry nodded in grim satisfaction. He reached for a soiled tea towel and began to dry his face.

Suddenly the station alarm began to ring.

As Harry, John and Ken were scrambling into their fire fighting gear beside the engine, Harry said, 'Typical.'

'What?'

'Bloody fire.'

'Amazing, isn't it? Us being firemen and all,' said Ken.

'Knock it off!'

But John played on. 'I've got this friend. He's a copper, and they keep getting rung up about crimes.'

'Yeah. Okay. Anyway, after tonight it's all yours, and you're welcome to it.' As they got into the engine

Harry suddenly remembered something. 'I didn't get my present. What is it?'

'A teasmade,' said John happily.

Harry paused and considered the situation carefully. 'A teasmade? Won't need it, mate. I'm going to wake up to a pina colada, slip on my Bermudas and wander down to the pool . . .'

'Listen to it!' scoffed Ken as the engine roared out of the station and down the street, traffic slowing and either getting out of – or getting into – its way.

Harry continued to bemoan his spoilt party as they tore their way through the early evening streets and the others nodded, thinking their own thoughts.

'Looks like a skip fire to me,' said Ken as they roared up to a building site.

The blaze had overflowed the skip and had set fire to some tarpaulin-covered wood. It was quite fierce and was now spreading towards the site hut. Ominously, several British Oxygen containers of oxyacetylene were propped up against the wooden walls. Harry took all this in as the engine screeched to a halt and the firemen jumped out.

As they started to unreel the hoses, Ken noticed the flames had just started dancing around the tanks and he tapped Harry urgently on the back. 'Come on – we haven't got any time.' Without waiting for Harry's reaction, Ken rushed forward to the site hut and began to tip the first of the tanks over. Harry quickly followed him and together they began to roll the containers away.

'What kept you?' Ken asked.

'I was frozen with terror,' Harry told him ironically.

'Look at 'em,' said John from a few yards away as he stood by a fireman splaying water over the skip. 'Talk about Butch Cassidy and the Sundance Kid.'

The hoseman glanced up with a mischievous look in his eyes. 'Shall I?'

'Why not?' John smiled sweetly at him. 'I think it's a good idea, don't you?'

'Super-duper,' said the hoseman as he raised the hose and changed its direction.

The spray drenched Ken and Harry who turned round in fury, gesticulating and cursing. Meanwhile their fire fighting colleagues burst into 'Raindrops keep falling on my head'. Reluctantly Ken and Harry put their arms round each others shoulders and, smiling wetly, joined in.

'You really want to go to Spain?' asked Ken in the pub that night.

Harry looked defensive. 'I got talked into it.'

'What I mean is, I can't imagine—'

'Yeah, all right. Neither can I. Now leave it out.'

'You'll be serving the coladas—'

'Not if I can help it.'

'So what you gonna do?'

'Buy a boat – when I've got the bar off the ground. Do a spot of fishing.'

'Then you *will* be serving pina coladas?'

'Temporarily.'

'So it's the wife's dream, is it?'

'Something like that.'

'We'll miss you.' Ken went to get another round. When he returned, he found Harry sitting there with tears in his eyes.

'Blimey – want to swop the beer for gin?'

'Mother's Ruin? No, I was just thinking – no more rest room, no more laughs—'

'There'll be a barrel of laughs on the Costa Brava.'

'Yeah.'

'Think of all those ex-pat Brits you'll meet.'

'You mean the dodgy ones?'

'All of 'em. It's an exile's paradise.'

'I'm not on the run, you know.' He buried his nose in his beer. 'Of course, I might be soon – from Spain, I mean.'

'It may not be as bad as all that.'

'Mm.'

'Could be a bit of a laugh.'

'Spanish food never agreed with me. I'll have permanent Montezuma's Revenge. Vomit every day. Get a paunch.'

'You've got one.'

'Improve it.' He drained his beer and got to his feet with a slight stagger. 'I'm gonna get pissed.'

'In Spain?'

'No, here and now.'

And get pissed they did with obvious enjoyment. At closing time, they rolled home together, singing dirty songs and yelling inane slurred war-cries. At Harry's front step they paused and spoke in exaggerated stage whispers.

'You'll come out.' Harry's voice was insistent.

'Where?'

'Spain.'

'Yeah – we'll get pissed on the local poison.'

'The vino?' Harry's voice broke. 'They don't even have any bleedin' bitter. And their beer – oh Gawd.'

'Import some.'

Harry brightened, just a fraction, and sat heavily down on the front step. 'Oh yeah?'

'The little red barrel in sunny Spain.'

'Mm.'

'Foaming tankards – just the right temperature.'

'Tepid. Difficult in the heat.'

'It's a challenge, Harry – your greatest challenge.' Ken was ponderous in his drunkenness. 'You'll climb it – and why—'

'Why?'

'Because it's there.'
'I'm not going climbing.'
'It's a manner of speaking.'
'Eh?'
Ken sat down beside him. 'So it's goodbye?'
Harry sniffed. 'It's goodbye.'
'I'll come out – if you get the beer right.'
'I'll miss you and the lads.' He sniffed again.
'We'll come out. Fireman's holiday.'
Harry cheered up. 'Now that would be something.'
'We'll paint the town.'
'Eh?'
'It's a manner of speaking.'
Harry began to laugh. 'We'll paint the town red,' he slurred. 'Show those bloody Spanish firemen.'
'Do they have 'em?'
'The Brigade.' Harry stood up, thinking he was still in the pub. He raised an imaginary glass. 'To the finest body of men in the world – the Brigade.'
Ken joined him and they stood in a drunken embrace, raising their imaginary glasses. Just then the door opened and Alison stood on the threshold, dressing-gowned, curlered and enraged.
'And what the hell do you two think you're doing?' she asked, arms akimbo.
'Putting out a fire,' said Harry as he staggered indoors.

Ken was in his shirt sleeves, working on his pride and joy – a white 650cc BSA A65 'Lightning'.
'I don't know why you bother with that wreck,' said John, coming up to him amicably and clapping him on the shoulder.
'It's a beautiful machine.'
'Just won't start.'
Ken shrugged, looking slightly hurt. 'You can't have everything, you know.'

'Anyway, grub's up,' said John. 'And there's a card from Harry.'

A few moments later Ken was reading aloud from the card which was pinned on the recreation room notice-board.

'"I have a dim memory of having worked with you pale people in a cold land." Thank you, Harry,' added Ken bitterly. '"Can't write any more. I have to turn on my stomach. Rosa is waiting with the oil. Adios. Harry."'

'Smug bastard,' said John. 'How does he get to run a bar in Spain?'

Ken took the card off the notice-board and looked at the picture which depicted an idyllic cove on the Costa Brava. 'I had one the same this morning.' He handed John an identical postcard. 'Nice, isn't it?'

'If you can get it,' replied John in a gloomy voice.

Ken and John were still discussing Harry's escape to the sun next morning over breakfast TV. Their colleagues seemed totally uninterested as they watched the flickering, jabbering screen.

'Well, he saved his pennies,' said Ken wistfully.

'And bought a bar in Spain,' agreed John between clenched teeth. 'He always was a mean sod.'

'I expect his missus kept him on line. After all, it was she who wanted the Spanish effort.'

'Yes,' said John, 'I admit she had a hand in it. But what I can't get over is—'

He was never to explain what he couldn't get over. The alarm was sounded and they stood up as one man and rushed from the room.

The fire-engine screeched to a halt in front of a house from which dark grey smoke was billowing. The crew leapt out and began to unroll the hoses while Ken and John ran to the house, only to stop dead in their tracks as a policeman burst out of the front door, a small boy in his arms.

'Anyone else?' asked Ken.

'Parents upstairs, I think,' replied the policeman, choking.

'What's the name?'

'It's too late, Ken,' said John quickly.

'Name!' rapped Ken.

'Roper,' returned the policeman.

'It'll go any second,' yelled John, but Ken was already rushing towards the front door. 'Ken. Ken! Come back! Don't be a bloody fool,' John bellowed after him. But Ken was not paying the slightest attention to John or anyone else as he tore through the smoke-filled house, calling out the Ropers' name.

'Bloody smokie!' John turned back to his colleagues. 'Okay – come on. Let's get the gear and get in there.'

Inside the house, the smoke was intense and Ken wheezed and coughed as he continued to call out the Ropers' name. But the situation was familiar enough for there were times in the past when he'd not had the time to pull on breathing apparatus. It was all a question of speed for both rescuers and victims.

Suddenly he thought he heard something and he stopped, gasping for air in the acrid, suffocating smoke. The muffled, desperate screaming momentarily became clearer and, choking, he followed it down the swirling blackness of the corridor. Soon he found himself up against a closed door. Instinctively he kicked hard at it – again and again – until it opened abruptly. The rush of air caused the flames to roar straight up at him and Ken covered his face as the searing heat bit hard.

It was at least three minutes, wearing their

breathing equipment, before they got to him – and it was John who dragged him slowly down the smoke-filled corridor and out of the doomed house.

Ken lay on the front path, his face blackened, only his eyes mobile amidst his stiffened features.

'He's a gonner,' said John helplessly, leaning over him whilst they radioed for an ambulance. 'He's a gonner.'

It was as if Ken was wearing a mask – some deadly black carnival mask. But the eyes were those of a wounded animal as they looked beseechingly up at John, who was trying hard to pull himself together.

Hesitantly he patted Ken on the shoulder of his charred uniform. 'You'll make it,' he said.

The ambulance roared down the dual carriageway, its siren screaming. In the swaying interior, John sat close to Ken who seemed to have lapsed into unconsciousness. His eyes were closed and his breathing was heavy, almost rasping. Will he make it? wondered John desperately. They were all used to taking necessary risks, to danger – but this didn't make it any easier when the worst happened. And now it had.

Ken was one of the best, John knew that, and he had resilience. Bags of it. The High Plains Drifter they called him. Partly because of his hobby – reading pulp Westerns – and partly because he was still a bachelor at thirty-seven. Liked by the ladies, Ken had never become involved with any particular girl long enough for her to catch him. He'd been in the West Midlands Fire Brigade for years and, in many ways, John considered, it was ideal for him. It was the perfect job for a Western hero – bacon and beans, night watches, companionship in danger, its glamour, its unassuming social value. And as for his horse – well, Ken had White Lightning – the BSA A65, a Birmingham Small Arms creation which had been built in the sixties. It had a top speed of 120 mph, but through lack of maintenance by previous owners the bike was now unreliable. Nevertheless, although White Lightning was often in bits in Ken's shed, he cherished his steed more than any woman.

The quiet, solitary stranger riding into town, thought John romantically. That's our Ken. But look at him now – charred and blackened and maybe dying. That's our hero. John turned away, unable to bear it any longer.

John looked through the glass window of the intensive care unit and gloomily watched Ken breathing in an oxygen tent. To say the least, he looked rough. Very rough.

'The burns are only superficial, you know,' said the young doctor, but John didn't know whether to believe him or not. 'They're minor,' continued the doctor firmly and John was suddenly cheered. Maybe Ken just looked worse than he actually was – maybe a miracle was happening.

'Terrific.' John was instantly pressing. 'So what? You reckon a week or two before we get him back?'

'On duty? I wouldn't be too optimistic about that just now. He inhaled with the blast. I'm afraid there's lung damage.'

'Oh no.' John's hopes plunged again. Why on earth couldn't they come out with it all at once – give him the complete picture.

The doctor continued almost unwillingly. 'It's hard as yet to know what the extent of the damage is. We'll find that out as soon as he's up and about.'

'Yes . . .' John was doubtful.

'And the boy's parents—'

‘Yes,’ cut in John, ashamed that he hadn’t enquired about them before, ‘how are the Ropers?’

‘Well, not exactly comfortable, but very, very lucky. If your friend hadn’t managed to open that door . . .’

‘Yes. He’s tough, is Ken.’

‘I hope so,’ said the doctor thoughtfully.

Ken had recovered consciousness slowly and as he came to the fuzzy images of doctor and nurses hardly made any impression on him at all. All he could remember was the smoke filling his lungs, the struggle to breathe and then nothing – nothing at all.

Then the pain caught up with him and for some days he was in agony. It was only when the young doctor came to see him that he felt initially reassured.

‘How are you?’ he had asked, sitting on the bed jauntily.

‘Rough.’

‘Those burns – they’re purely superficial.’

‘And they’re purely bloody sore.’

‘They will be for a bit.’

‘And then they’ll be all right?’

‘They’ll be all right.’

They stared at each other for a moment and Ken could see that the doctor had lost his jauntiness and was looking vaguely uneasy.

‘Got something to tell me?’

‘Well—’

‘My breathing’s bad. That’ll go, won’t it?’

‘It’ll improve.’

‘But—’

‘You’ve got lung damage. Nothing that serious. But – a bit of a problem.’

Ken sighed. ‘Just a bit?’

'Absolutely nothing to worry about.' The doctor seemed happier now it was all in the open.

'You're sure about that?'

'Bit of puffing and panting, that's all.'

When he had gone, Ken lay back on the bed and relaxed. I've been bloody lucky, he thought. Bit of puffing and panting. If that's all there is to it, I'm laughing.

It was not until he was wired up to a running machine that he realised the full extent of the damage to his lungs. What the doctor had described as 'slight lung damage – bit of a problem', suddenly seemed much worse. He soon realised that he could no way match the pace he knew he should have been able to keep up, and was all too conscious of the medical supervisor noting his decline on his clipboard. Another supervisor turned the machine off and Ken collapsed, gasping.

'My Gawd,' he panted. 'That was bad, wasn't it?'

'You're doing very well,' said a brisk nurse. 'You're a lucky man.'

'Lucky?'

'Come on now,' she said, bearing down on him. 'We've got to get back to bed. Mustn't tire ourselves, must we?'

That afternoon Ken was back in the hospital ward, hopelessly depressed. The full implications of his lung problem were beginning to come home to him and John didn't exactly help when he appeared at visiting time. Admittedly he came armed with Ken's favourite Westerns, but he was also in a funereal mood as he sat on the end of the bed.

'It looks bad, Ken.'

'Bollocks!' He began to cough.

'Come on. You didn't even get through the hospital tests. D'you think you'd pass ours?'

'Look, I told you. I did those tests too soon. I explained that to you. I accept that.' But Ken knew his tone of voice was all too defensive.

'It's not me, Ken.'

'Superman would struggle on those machines . . .'

'Listen, mate, we've been through a lot together.'

Suddenly Ken realised how serious John was. Maybe he wasn't just being depressing – maybe he was being realistic. With a struggle, he tried for rationality.

'Okay, you're saying I can't do the business any more. Right?'

'You failed a basic fitness test . . .'

'No, okay. Put me on the next station drill.'

'Look, Ken . . .'

'That's fair enough, isn't it? A real test –, on the ground. Not those bloody machines. If I do it I've shown something; if I don't then there's no argument – in front of the lads and whoever else . . . What's wrong with that?'

John shook his head. 'I can't do it. Not just like that.'

Ken interrupted him. 'Don't write me off, okay? I'm a smokie and I always will be. I can still kick your arse.'

'Right,' said John dutifully.

'Set it up, John.'

'Okay.' He was obviously unwilling.

'I know what you're thinking. Well, we'll just see. We'll just see.' Ken lay back on his bed and began to cough again.

In the end, however unwilling he was, John was as good as his word. Two weeks later, Ken recovered from his superficial burns and was discharged from the hospital. Unable to bear the tension and the tedium of waiting, he presented himself at the station and, characteristically, demanded that the test should be run.

'You sure you're ready?' demured John, but Ken was insistent.

'You trying to edge me out?' he said aggressively.

'No,' said John. 'I just think it's crazy trying something like this when you're meant to be recuperating.'

The rest of White Watch agreed. 'Don't do it, mate,' said Bill Tyson, and Bobby Preston took him aside.

'Don't be such a bloody fool.'

'I'm as good as I'll ever be.'

'You're not. You need rest.'

'I can do it.'

'Sure you can – in time. No one just gets out of hospital and jumps into action.'

'Ken Boon does.'

'Who do you think you are – Superman?'

'I think I can do it.'

'I don't.' Bobby turned back to the rest of White Watch. 'Lads, talk him out of it. Tell him he's a wally.'

A babble of enthusiastic voices told him he was and gave Ken a dozen different reasons for not going through with the test. But Ken wasn't listening and he silenced them with an angry shout.

'Are you trying to tell me something?'

'Yeah,' said John, 'like you shouldn't do it. Like we should wait.'

'Bollocks!'

'Don't be a fool.'

'I reckon you're trying to get rid of me – and get me out.' Ken was angry and defensive. He was also rather frightened, for the emotion was already making him wheeze slightly. 'I'm going through with it. Now.'

'All right,' said John.

'And no one's gonna bleedin' stop me.'

'No,' said John patiently. 'No one's gonna bleedin' stop you.' He led Ken outside, followed by the rest of White Watch. The men were subdued, no longer their usual noisy, boisterous selves.

'We're going to watch an execution,' muttered one of them as they gathered in front of the practice tower. The day was overcast, with an edgy wind that scattered waste paper depressingly across the yard.

'You fit, Ken?' John was wary, unable to bear what was going to happen.

'I'm fit,' said Ken and began to climb the mechanical ladder.

Within seconds what John had feared so much came about. Ken was wheezing. Nevertheless, with gathering leadenness he managed to climb, clinging to the top, trying desperately to get his breath back.

'Poor sod,' whispered John.

Slowly and painfully Ken climbed back to the ground. Then he almost staggered across to the next part of the test – a large sack. Gasping, he struggled to get it on his back – and just made it. John winced as Ken began to run; he could see the sheer will-power etched on his face. Then he faltered, paused, fought for air, started to run again – and collapsed.

As White Watch ran towards him, Ken heaved himself up on one elbow and wheezed, 'All right, you bastards. You know I'm finished.'

John knelt down beside him. 'I told you to wait.'

Ken swore at him fulsomely. Then he grinned. 'I'll wait.'

Over the next six months, Ken took another test – and then another. But it was no good; he failed both. True, each time he was a little fitter, but his lungs continuously let him down. Eventually the top brass saw him, sympathetically and respectfully. They pensioned him off, and Ken went to the pub with John, mortified and depressed.

'Eighteen years – and I'm grounded. Doesn't bear thinking about.'

'Why don't you go out to Spain and join Harry? He'd be glad of your company.'

'Yeah – we'd be pissed every night. No thanks. And besides, there's Alison.'

'What's wrong with Alison?'

'You know what she's like. We wouldn't get on.'

'You could both try.'

'We'd both fail. Honest.'

'So—'

Ken took a long pull of his beer. 'Out in the bloody cold,' he said.

'You've got a pension – and you're still a young man. You could get a job – security maybe – and have your pension.'

Ken frowned. 'Sure – put out to grass. Like some old crock. I'm not working for any security firm.'

'Consultant? Advisor?'

'No, I'm not sitting behind a desk.'

John sighed. 'Have you got *any* plans?'

'Oh yes,' said Ken, surprising him. 'I've got plans all right.'

Chapter Three

Ken breathed in deeply. Two months had passed since he had left the fire brigade – two months of alienation and a growing sense of isolation. Yet because of the idea – the crazy, attractive fulfilling idea – Ken had survived. Now, as he stood beside the estate agent's SOLD sign, he gazed with loving attention at the field he had bought. He had already enclosed it with a small white picket fence and placed a small caravan in the middle. Ken had laboured long and hard but he knew his problems were just beginning. The only thing he didn't know was the size of them.

The idea of going it alone, building his house and surrounding it with a smallholding, had grown slowly as he grimly realised he was never going to pass the fitness test. It was the only thing he could do. An ordinary job would be anathema after the Service and Ken baulked at the dullness it would bring into his life. He had always been a loner and had dreamed, in his Western fantasies, of striking out West, building his own half-timbered shack and living off the land. Well – he glanced around him – a field in the West Midlands wasn't the same, but it was a start.

A truck drew up outside and hooted. Cheerfully Ken waved it through the gate and it stopped by the caravan. The driver and his mate got out and grunted at him.

'All right?'

'Fine,' said Ken. 'What've we got today?'

The driver consulted his clipboard and then gave it to Ken to check. 'Breeze blocks, sand and cement, roofing slates. Okay?'

'Shall I sign?' said Ken.

'Boss said cash.'

There was a short uncomfortable pause. 'Come on,' said Ken impatiently, 'does he think I've got that much cash lying about?'

'Don't tell me.'

'I'll give you a cheque.'

'You'll have to give me – hang on –' He looked down at the clipboard and began to count. 'Let me see . . . four plus . . . You'll have to give me five cheques, mate. Sorry.'

'You're joking.'

'You want to work for him.'

'Hang on.' Ken hurried into his caravan and the driver nodded to his mate. As they started to unload, Ken sat signing five cheques – and cursing. It definitely wasn't going to be easy.

A few days later Ken was heaving sacks of cement into position. He was sweating, wheezing, yet determined to keep going somehow. On the gate a small sign had been painted. It read 'Ponderosa'.

Wheezing more heavily than before, Ken leant against the gate, thankful for the rest. As he gazed down the road he saw a van approaching, with a familiar face at the wheel. It was Harry. But why the hell wasn't he in Spain?

'Hallo, Smokie!' said Harry, jumping innocently out of the van. He wasn't very tanned, but was rather paunchy.

Ken was delighted to see him. 'You bastard! What are you doing here?'

'What do you mean what am I doing here? I've come to see you, fat face!'

'But what are you doing here?' Ken insisted.

Harry wasn't coming clean so fast. 'Talk about bloody interrogation! Make us some tea. Have you got a kettle, or do you drink rainwater?'

'Stick it.' Ken paused, 'You look great.'

'So do you. How are things?'

'Brilliant,' said Ken firmly. 'You?'

'Never better.'

'What's this then?' said Ken, poking at Harry's stomach.

Harry heaved his stomach in defensively. 'Paella,' he replied.

'How's Alison?'

Harry shrugged and abruptly changed the subject. 'Okay. I went to see the boys this morning. They said you'd be here.'

'They were right.' He wondered if Harry knew how much he missed White Watch – it was like losing a family.

'They were moaning you don't keep in touch.'

'Well, it's a new life here.' He looked down at the ground. 'I wanted to get a bit sorted out first . . . Have a breathe of this air, Harry. Fantastic, eh?'

Harry dutifully snorted in and out. 'Smashing. You breathing all right, are you?' He looked at Ken in concern.

'Fine. Come on, let's have that tea.'

Ken put the kettle on whilst Harry sat down heavily on the unmade bunk.

'So you've gone and bought a field. Bloody idiot.'

'It's not a field,' said Ken sharply, handing him a milky cup of tea.

'What else do you call a bit of flat grass?'

'It's what it will be, not what it is now. Imagine greenhouses, Harry, and a big house with a verandah, and lots of tomatoes and, well, you know, all sorts of veggies.' His voice had taken on a hectoring tone.

'You were always potty about vegetables, but this is going a bit far.'

'I'll do it.'

'What with?'

'I'll do it. It's what I want.'

'You're not lonely out here?'

'No.'

'I don't know why you didn't get another job. A wage packet and a pension: you'd have been well set up.'

'Try getting work with a medical record.'

'Nice van,' said Harry, looking round him. 'All the mod cons. What did you do? Buy it or is it on hire or what?'

'Well, I think I've bought it. I've just got to persuade the bank that I have.'

Harry looked meaningfully at a pile of receipts and invoices. 'Doing your bills?'

'Weighing them . . . What happened to your tan, Harry?'

'Faded.'

'I thought you were supposed to get sun all the year round.'

There was a long silence. 'I've come home, Ken. For good.'

Ken didn't look surprised. 'Have you? I was wondering.'

'By myself.'

'What happened?'

'Oh I dunno, mate, I got dumped. I was . . .' He paused. 'Dumped is the only word I can think of at the moment.'

'Alison's left you?'

'Yeah.'

'I'm sorry, Harry.'

'It's all right – I'm not worried.' But he very clearly was. 'She changed out there, Ken. She just changed.'

'How?'

'Bloody unfair – she seemed to get younger. Know what I mean?'

'And you?'

'I felt me age. The heat brought it out, I think. I just lumbered about.'

'Was the bar a success?'

'Oh yeah – I did a lot of renovations and now it's swinging away.'

'Who was behind the bar?'

'Alison – originally. Then me.'

'You?' Ken was surprised.

'She had better things to do.'

'I see.' Ken shook his head. 'She always was restless.'

'I didn't fit in. They're all gigolos out there.'

'Oh yeah?'

'I hated the climate too,' said Harry reflectively. 'Couldn't find a decent drizzle anywhere. No draughts, no blizzards . . . Terrible place.'

'Must have been torture. Of course there was the cheap booze . . .'

Harry ignored him. 'The worst thing is she's gone off with a bloody hairdresser – he's about fourteen. It's a disgrace. She'll come to her senses and then we'll bloody see.' He looked miserably at the blank face of the large TV set that dominated the interior of the caravan. There was a long pause and then he turned to Ken again. 'John said you can't run or anything. Is that true?'

Ken was instantly furiously defensive. 'Is that what he said? He said that to you!'

'He was sad about it,' said Harry reasonably.

'John can sod off. I can run. I can do anything. He can sod off.' He swallowed angrily, trying to regain control.

'It's great to see you.' Harry's voice was genuine.

'You too. Bugger 'em all, eh?'

'Absolutely.'

'What you going to do with yourself?' He sounded a little more cheerful now. 'Fancy a spot of gardening?'

'I've got a hotel.' There was a stunned silence.

'Have you? What? Here?'

Harry nodded. 'Smashing place. Bags of potential.'

'Is it standing up?'

'I'm serious. I sold up over there. At a good profit too. And this place is all right. Come and see me. Come and stay.'

'Okay,' said Ken, but both of them knew that he hadn't the slightest intention of doing so.

'I want to get the AA over to see it by the end of the year. Couple of stars. I'm on the map.'

'So we're both all right.'

'Yeah.'

The doubt in their voices was all too clear. There was another long silence until, distantly, a telephone began to ring.

'Where is it?' asked Harry in confusion.

'You passed it,' replied Ken. 'It's out by the gate.' He hurried out, leaving Harry contemplating their mutual plight.

Ken set out briskly for the phone box at the end of the lane, but even at a fast walk he was getting puffed. Eventually he made it, pulling the door open and grabbing at the receiver. But for a few seconds he couldn't speak for lack of breath.

'Mr Boon?'

'Yeah.' Ken managed to splutter out the word.

'This is Mr Fowler – your building material supplier.'

'Yeah.'

'Er – I'm afraid to say that one of your cheques has bounced.' His tone was reasonable but insistent. 'I thought we agreed that you'd only write out fifty pounds per cheque.'

'I did.'

'When was that?'

'The other day. I did about half a dozen cheques for one delivery. It's like writing a flipping book each time. So I suggest you resubmit. I spoke to the bank and they were quite happy to—'

But Mr Fowler was not happy with his bland reassurance. 'I have resubmitted, Mr Boon. And the cheque's been returned.'

'That's ridiculous. He definitely—'

'I'm sorry, Mr Boon.' There was a new and steely note in Fowler's voice. 'I'd like you to come down to the office straightaway.'

'But I'm—'

'Straightaway!'

'Yes, Mr Fowler,' said Ken humbly. 'I'll be there.' He put the phone down feeling beaten and walked slowly back to the caravan. There he found Harry sitting disconsolately on the step.

'You're not going?'

'I've got a hotel to run.'

'What about another cup of tea?'

'Next time. I left the address.'

'Yeah.'

'Come any time. There'll always be a room and a bottle.'

'I'll drop in.'

Harry looked up at him curiously. 'You look a bit down. That call okay?'

'The call?' repeated Ken. 'Yes, the call. It was nothing.'

'See you.'

'You take care,' said Ken with sudden fondness.

Harry got into the van and reversed up the lane. Ken watched him go miserably and then turned back to Ponderosa – the field of his dreams. His future. But it was more like a battlefield.

The bank crisis – and Ken's inability to solve his cash-flow problems – plunged him further into despair over the next few days. He had always been used to a regular salary and the longer he spent with his calculator and the increasing pile of bills, the more complex the situation seemed to become. The gap between the constraints of his brigade pension and the long period before Ponderosa would earn any money at all seemed to be becoming wider and wider. And with this realisation his dreams of self-sufficiency were growing dimmer. Inevitably, his physical work was marred by his condition and he seemed to be sliding into a state of chaos. His accounts were in a mess, his health not up to the efforts required – everything was becoming a vicious circle. And in addition he was lonely – desperately lonely. Then matters came to an unpleasant head.

Ken was asleep in a half-made bed, the caravan untidy around him. A Zane Grey novel was half open on his chest and he slept fitfully, wheezing slightly. Suddenly, unbelievably, the caravan began to shake, causing books and ornaments to topple onto his bunk. He woke to see the group photograph of White Watch shaking unsteadily, and he sat up with a start as a picture fell to the floor with a crash. After a few seconds of incomprehension, Ken leapt out of bed to investigate. Wearing a coat over his pyjamas and dragging on a pair of wellington boots, he stepped out blearily only to find men attempting to move the caravan off its stabilisers.

'What the bloody hell are you playing at?' he asked, still amazed.

'What does it look like?'

'You can just bugger off.'

'Who's been a naughty boy, then? Not paid his bills.'

'What?'

Fowler suddenly appeared from his Landrover, which was parked over by the fence.

'What's all this then?' asked Ken, his heart sinking.

'I think you know, Mr Boon. Don't let's have any trouble now.'

'Can you tell your men to leave my van alone, please?' He struggled to put authority into his voice – and failed.

'*My* van, I think you mean, Mr Boon.' Fowler brandished some documents. 'For the second week running your instalment has bounced. I did warn you.' He ended on a note of insufferable smugness.

'It's a mistake.'

'You've told me that before.'

'Okay?' asked one of the workmen, looking up at Fowler for permission to continue.

'Leave that, friend, unless you want a thick ear!' Ken's voice was becoming more aggressive now.

'Let's not be unreasonable.'

'Now look! I'm woken up by these idiots attacking my van.' He shook his head. 'I don't think that's reasonable.'

But Fowler wasn't having any. 'I'm returning your cheque and you must return my caravan.'

'How can I? I've got nowhere to live.'

'Build your house.'

'I intend to. I just need a bit more time. It's only a cash-flow problem. It's not—'

'We've all got cash-flow problems. I've got a business to run – men to pay.'

'Too right,' put in the workman.

'Can you get rid of this bloke? He's really getting

on my wick.' Ken took a step towards him and Fowler sighed.

'What are we going to do with you, Mr Boon?'

Ken tried to be reasonable. 'Look, I'm sure I can get money to you by the end of the week.'

Fowler thought, then he said slowly, 'Friday morning?'

'Friday. Saturday . . .'

'By Friday morning.'

'Okay.'

'Cash. All the arrears. No more discussions.'

'Fair enough.' Ken sounded uneasy.

'Come on then, lads,' said Fowler with sudden decision, and with reluctance his two workmen began to retreat. Fowler ambled away himself, turning back at the Landrover. 'By Friday morning,' he repeated threateningly.

'Friday morning it is,' said Ken with a confidence he did not feel. Then, when he was sure his unwelcome visitors had left, Ken turned slowly back to his caravan. Once inside, he lay on his rumpled bed in despair, unable to sleep, unable to see anything but a very bleak future. Then, as the grey dawn rolled over Ponderosa, he had an idea.

Next morning, Ken's mind was made up. There was no other decision he could take. His only transport nowadays was the beaten-up old Lightning, so buttoning up his belstaff jacket and donning his brimless skid-lid, he mounted it, started up with difficulty and spluttered away over the field. The bike sounded like Ken himself – in need of attention.

The Grand Hotel was not quite as Harry had described it. A Victorian building that had seen better days, the hotel was undergoing an extensive exterior paint job.

Ken parked his bike and walked through the front

entrance, where polythene-wrapped 'easy chairs' lay around in a jumbled heap. Nick, the ancient resident all-purpose porter, was struggling with one of the chairs. Ken followed him through to the small reception area and caught up with him just as he collapsed into the chair.

'"Easy chairs" they call 'em,' he confided in Ken. 'I'd call 'em a bloody pain in the arse!' He began to cough dramatically. 'I'll never fetch the rest in,' he said.

'Want a hand?'

'Could do with one.'

Ken slowly walked back to the entrance, and then returned, struggling with another chair. As he came back, Doreen Evans, Harry's part-time receptionist, emerged from the office. She was in her early thirties, attractive, well-dressed – and under the impression that Ken was delivering the chairs.

'I'd rather you hadn't put them there actually.' She turned to Nick. 'I did say in the lounge, Nick.'

'Sorry,' said Ken humbly, deciding to play along with his new role.

'Have you got your invoice?' she asked him briskly. 'One dozen easy chairs.'

'I hope so.'

'Can I ask you to move them now. We're open now and they're a bit of an eyesore.'

'Do you want them all in here?'

She shrugged. 'That'll be fine.' Doreen walked hurriedly away to the bar, but not without Ken's appraising glance.

'Thanks, mate,' said Nick with heartfelt gratitude.

'I'll go and put the kettle on,' called Doreen. 'Tea or coffee?'

'Anything. Tea will do.'

'When you've finished Nick'll bring you through to the kitchen. Just mention tea and he'll revive suddenly.' She smiled and headed off in the direction of the kitchen.

After all the daunting physical labour at Ponderosa, Ken was delighted to find lifting the chairs comparatively easy and he soon had the task completed with scarcely a wheeze. He then wandered into the kitchen to find Nick the porter getting a pasting from Ethel. She was a tough-looking character, somewhere in her sixties, and appeared to be a kind of domestic factotum.

'It's a never-ending tunnel, your mouth,' she was telling Nick. 'Anyway, it's brewed.'

'I only said we're gasping.'

'And you should make your own tea. You're not helpless.'

'I've slogged myself stupid. You want to go outside and look.' He turned to Ken. 'I'm not a man, I'm a beast of burden. Everybody disappears in this place soon as there's work to do.'

'God forgive you,' Ethel commented.

'Thanks,' said Ken, sitting down. 'Just the job.'

Just then, Doreen came in and once again Ken gave her that cool, appraising glance.

'Nick,' she reprimanded, 'in a minute you should really get the wrapping off those chairs and set them out properly.'

'I've just sat down,' he complained. 'See what I mean?' he said to Ken.

'Is Harry about?'

'Mr Crawford? Why? Is there a problem with the delivery?'

'Was there?' Ken asked Nick.

'Don't think so.'

'You see, Mr Crawford is out at the moment. Can I help?'

'No. Just tell him Ken dropped by to say hallo. We're old friends.'

Doreen looked at him in some surprise, but before she could speak, Harry appeared. He looked almost ecstatic.

'I know that voice,' he cried as he came into the kitchen armed with supplies from the Cash and Carry. 'Ken! Hallo, mate!' He wrung Ken's hand and the whole kitchen seemed bathed in the warmth of his affection.

'Hallo, Harry. All right?'

'Make yourself at home, then.' He turned to Nick. 'Nick, get the rest of the stuff out of the van, eh? Doreen, this is Ken Boon, my mate from the White Watch.'

'Oh, I thought . . .'

'The chap with the field?' asked Nick incredulously.

'Market garden,' said Harry quickly, with sudden embarrassment.

'In the making,' added Ken to let him off the hook.

'This is Doreen, Ken. She's my right-hand man.'

'I only sound female,' she said sourly.

'And this is Ethel. Ken here can tell you a few stories about me.'

'Just a few.'

'What do you think of my place, then, eh?' Harry suddenly looked agitated.

'Chairs are nice.'

'They're just the start.'

'Listen,' said Doreen. 'I'm sorry about – before.' She was clearly anxious to make amends.

'No, it was my fault.'

'I thought Ken was the delivery man,' she told Harry by way of slightly embarrassed explanation.

'He just doesn't dress well,' said Harry tolerantly. 'Any chance of a cuppa, Ethel?'

'Did you remember the bleach while you were out shopping?' she asked him severely.

'You won't believe this – I've forgotten it again,' said Harry penitently.

Ethel wearily handed him a cup of tea. 'I can. Here you are, but you don't deserve it.'

'I know.' He turned to Doreen. 'Those painters. They clocked off already?'

She nodded sadly.

'Turn your back for five minutes . . . Where's Nick got to now?' Suddenly they realised he'd drifted away. 'Nick comes with the hotel,' Harry told Ken. 'Part of the fixtures and fittings.'

'He's Victorian,' added Doreen.

'That's right,' said Harry reflectively. 'So come on, mate, guided tour of the palace. Bring your tea.'

Ken got up. 'Okay.'

'Come on. Or do we have to treat you like an old crock?'

'Not yet,' said Ken as he got to his feet. 'Not quite yet.'

'This is the dining-room,' Harry said. 'I haven't done much in here yet, but I've plans for a breakfast patio with some tiles and stuff – nice wrought-iron trellis work. The Spanish influence. What do you think?'

'Tremendous.'

'Of course, the food's the thing. Good food and people will eat it off the floor. Ethel's a bloody marvel. You all right, mate?'

'I'm fine, yeah. Wondered if we could have a chat actually, Harry?'

'A chat? I want a biography, mate!' Harry propelled him out of the dining-room and into the small bar. 'Do you like the place?'

'I do.'

'Think it's got potential?'

'Bags of it.'

'Now I'm going to extend this bar. Once that's

done I'm serving –' He broke off as he saw Nick busy setting out the armchairs in serried rows as if they were all watching an invisible television. 'It's not an aeroplane, Nick,' said Harry edgily. 'This is a place to relax. You don't want someone's knees up your backside.'

Nick sourly started re-choreographing the chairs.

'We'll come back later and rehearse people drinking,' said Harry, propelling Ken back to the reception area.

Before Harry could continue to talk about his renovation plans, Ken said, 'There was something I particularly wanted to ask you about.'

Harry was immediately receptive and Ken felt an onrush of warmth for him.

'Right. Let's go and sit in the office. Doreen's there but I don't keep anything from her. She's divorced as well: we understand each other. She doesn't fancy me, but she does my VAT, which is the next best thing.'

But Ken was reluctant to bare his soul in front of Doreen. 'Some other time will do.'

'No problem. You want to talk in private you can. Course you can.' He led the way through to the office and Ken reluctantly followed him. Was he doing the right thing? he wondered. Or shouldn't he just go back to Ponderosa and get on with it? Then he thought of the jumbled pile of bills on the table in the caravan, of the bank, of Fowler – and suddenly he was desperate to talk to Harry.

Harry opened the office door and said to Doreen, 'Can we turn you out of here for a few moments?'

'Of course.'

'Sorry,' said Ken humbly.

She flashed him a smile. 'No problem. Anyway, I'm still red-faced about earlier so . . .'

'You've never been red-faced in your life,' put in Harry.

'You'd be surprised. See you later.' She went out but must have heard Harry say, 'Smashing, eh?'

'Seems to be.'

'Saving my life on the money front. She's like a hawk, honestly, doesn't miss a thing. Tortures me for receipts, makes me get quotes. Astonishing. She's going to be a croupier – she's training. The casinos'll snap her up. I'll have to nail her to the floor.' He pulled himself together abruptly. 'Okay. Shut up, Harry. I'm all ears, mate.'

Ken began hesitantly. 'Well . . .'

'Sit down, Ken.'

He numbly did as he was told. 'Harry, I'm broke. Not broke, uh . . . I'm . . . I haven't got any money at the minute and I'm . . . it's a cash-flow thing.'

Harry was instantly sympathetic. 'Don't tell me. This place is a sponge. It's incredible. Shall I tell you how much I paid for these chairs? You'd be staggered. It's shocking.'

'I need about three hundred pounds, or else I lose the caravan.'

'That bad? Dear – oh – dear. Have you spoken to your bank?'

'I've spoken to everyone.'

'Ken, if I had three hundred quid I'd give it to you like a shot.'

Ken immediately rose to his feet, his hopes dashed. 'Sorry if I've . . .'

'No,' said Harry. There was a long pause. Then he muttered again, 'No.'

'I'd better get on then.'

'Listen, why don't you stay here? There's a bed here, number four, first floor. Easy climb.'

'Thanks, but I'd . . . I have to find some money.'

'Well, don't do anything daft,' said Harry inadequately, following the subdued Ken out of the office.

'No,' he replied bleakly, 'I won't.'
'What will you do?'
'Go home and have a think.'
'Have a think here,' said Harry encouragingly.
'No thanks, mate. I didn't want charity, I wanted to borrow money. Which I'd repay. Anyway . . .'
He began to buckle on his helmet.
'Stay for a drink. Don't just rush off.'
'No, I'll get back. Ta.'
Harry followed Ken out of the hotel and onto the street where the battered motorbike was parked. Ken tried to start the machine but nothing happened. He tried again and again whilst Harry watched gloomily.
'You could stay for a drink . . . wouldn't kill you.'
Still the bike refused to start. Ken sat astride it, a little puffed – wholly desperate.
'Same old bike, eh?'
With sudden decision Harry turned and walked into the hotel. 'I'll pull you a pint,' he said.
Slowly Ken dismounted and followed.

It was predictable they'd get drunk. Ken was in despair and Harry didn't know how to help him. So they got drunk and talked about old times, happily wrangling over the facts.
'That is not what happened.'
'It bloody is.'
'I went in. I was perfectly polite . . . *You*! *You* said it was a heart attack and needed the kiss of life!' Ken's voice was very slurred.
'It was you, mate. You said this budgie had popped off and needed resuscitation.'
'Bollocks!'
'You lying sod. You put – I swear, I swear – you put the oxygen mask on that bird and blew it out the window.'

'I can't believe you're saying this.' Ken had all the obsessive authority of a dead drunk. 'I'm going to ring John up. *You* said, "Look he's much better now, love, he's flown away."'

'Not only are your lungs buggered, mate, it's gone to your head.'

'I like budgies. I'd never harm a budgie.'

'It was dead.'

They laughed loud and long while Harry poured out more whisky. He went to look for the ice and found there wasn't any, so he took the bucket with him into the kitchen.

'He's much better now . . . he's flown away,' repeated Harry as he stumbled about the dark kitchen, opening the fridge and belching. In his attempts to extricate the ice tray he knocked a couple of eggs on to the floor. He didn't notice the damage, however, and blithely swayed back into the lounge, the ice tray clenched in his hand.

The drunken conversation continued as Ken and Harry discussed life, love and the fire-service.

'I loved it,' slurred Ken.

But Harry could not agree. 'I couldn't stand it. I couldn't wait to get out.'

'It was about something.'

'Don't be bloody mental. It wasn't about anything other than putting fires out. It's a stupid life and it buggered us both up.'

'No it didn't.'

'Oh, come on.'

'My lungs? No, my own fault. Stupid. Nothing to do with the service.'

'Listen to him. This is a man who put all his money into a field. Are the two things connected I ask myself? And I come up with an answer which is not "no". Ken . . . Ken . . .'

'You can't blame the service for your marriage

going wrong. And stop calling it a bloody field, will you?'

'Sorry. It is a field, but I will call it flat grass from now on. How is your flat grass? My wife left me because she – now this is complicated – she left me because she met me too late, and then decided she didn't like me because I was middle-aged. Because she didn't really know me properly when I was in the service. I was never around. Ask yourself why you never had a proper thing, with anybody.'

'I'm sorry but I think –' Ken ponderously searched for what he meant. 'Imagine this point is right and this point is completely wrong. Completely right; completely wrong. You are here.'

'Get a job, mate. That's your trouble.'

'Don't start, Harry. There aren't any jobs for a dud man.'

'I'll get the evening paper.'

'There are jobs, but I'm talking about . . . I've been for jobs. I could pump petrol. I could clean windows. I could skivvy. We've – 'cos you are completely wrong about this – we've had a real job. We saved lives.' There was a slight pause.

'Yeah. Babies waved to us from prams as we went by.'

'I get a few quid and the chance to open doors for a living. No thanks.'

'I'm not complaining. Don't include me.'

'I didn't say you were.'

'Because I'm not. I've got this place, eh?' Harry was becoming aggressive.

'It's not the Savoy.'

'No. I didn't say it was. Have you been to the Savoy?'

'No.'

'Then how do you know? That's the point.'

'Have you?'

'No. You come back here in a year and there'll be two stars above the front door. That is my prediction. Finish. And now I will get the evening newspaper and get you a job.'

'I've got one. I'm working for myself. I've got a market garden . . .'

'Without a market. You've got some flat grass and you need a job. And I will find you a job. End of subject. What do you want? Indoors or outdoors?'

'Yeah . . . if you think it's so easy, why don't you find me a job? A proper job for an ex-fireman, not an ex-road sweeper. You can't, can you? Can you?'

'I can. Yes I can.'

'I want three hundred pounds.'

'There are pages of jobs – pages,' said Harry, scanning the columns of the evening paper.

'Anyway, I don't want a job. All right? Clear? I need some money, and then I can go back to my job, which is to make a market garden. So shut up, Harry, will you?'

'Excuse me a moment, please. I have had an inspiration.' Harry staggered to his feet, stood for an instant in shaky dignity and then went hurriedly out. He managed to reach his office and sit down behind the desk. By now it was nearly midnight and he was finding it difficult to get his hands round the phone. He misdialled, cursed, and tried again. This time he got what he wanted – the *Evening Mail* answering machine. In his fuddled state he began to talk to it and then realised his mistake.

'Bloody machines. I hate these bloody things.' He replaced the receiver abruptly and hunted about for a pen. After a few minutes he inspected what he had written, nodded approval and dialled the answer-phone again. His voice, although over-articulated, sounded reasonably sober. 'Message is as follows. Sorry, credit card number is as follows: 4929 864 353

776 H. Crawford, Grand Hotel – you probably don't need that. Anyway, message is as follows: it's in the wanted column, for the jobs wanted list, all right? Big letters: EX-FIREMAN SEEKS INTERESTING WORK. Small letters: anything legal considered. No job too small. Box number. That's all. End of message. Um . . . goodnight.' He put the receiver down, belched, and made his way unsteadily back to Ken. Arms round each other's shoulders they staggered up the stairs and went to bed.

Chapter Four

Ken woke with a splitting headache after a nightmarish sleep in which he had dreamt of continuous pursuit. He had seen his caravan burnt by a triumphant Fowler and his field dug up by his workmen. He had even seen his own stumbling, breathless body being chased around and around the field until he was just marking time – and wheezing desperately.

'Ken.'

'All right,' he whispered, still asleep. 'I'll go – I'll go.'

'Ken.' The voice was insistent. 'It's Harry.'

'Eh?' Ken groaned and began to surface. Opening his eyes, he saw Harry standing over him with a tray. On the tray was a cup of tea, a large glass of Alka Seltzer and a small slip of paper.

'Good afternoon,' said Harry.

Ken groaned again.

'Some boys can take the pace and some boys can't,' said Harry smugly.

'What's going on?'

'The day is going on, my son. And it's liver for lunch. Make you feel better?'

'No.'

'I feel great.'

'Good.'

'Great, right. Anyway, you slack off, Boon. Some of us have got things to do. Some of us have been up since seven a.m.'

'Some of us wish some others of us would go away for a bit.'

'I brought you a cup of tea.'

'Leave the tea.'

'Thanks,' said Harry ironically.

Ken examined the tray which Harry had dumped on him. There was a cheque on it.

'What the hell's this?'

'What does it look like? It's a cheque.'

'No thanks, Harry.'

'It's only a hundred pounds, mate. That's all I can spare. It's not enough, but—'

'No.'

'I want it back. I'm first in the queue.'

'No, it's really . . .' He sighed. 'I know you haven't got it. Thanks.'

'Shut your mouth and take it, obstinate so-and-so.'

Ken shook his head firmly and groaned in the process.

'Drink your tea.'

He went out, leaving Ken staring at the cheque. He drank the Alka Seltzer, choked, sipped the tea – and choked again.

Half an hour later Ken limped into the kitchen, only to be instantly reprimanded by Ethel.

'You're in my bad books and no mistake,' she announced.

'Am I?' asked Ken meekly, his head pounding.

'The state of this kitchen this morning.'

'The state of me this morning. I'm in *my* bad books. Sorry, Ethel.'

She obviously relented but spoke just as fiercely. 'Eat something. Get food down you. It settles or it brings it up.'

'I'll suffer thanks.'

At that moment Doreen came in, looking even more attractive than ever. 'Hallo.'

'Mm,' said Ken.

'Oh dear – you are in a state.' Ken smiled grimly and Doreen continued, 'Reunion, eh?'

'Who needs them?'

She nodded vigorously. 'Have you seen Harry? I'm avoiding him. He's just had a set-to with the painters. They rolled up at one p.m. I think Harry's suggesting they roll off again, or words to that effect.' She turned to Ethel. 'Any chance of seconds for number eight? You should eat something,' she told Ken. 'You'll feel better.'

'I think what I will do is just go outside and chop my head off.'

He got up as Nick came in with the new edition of the *Mail*. 'There you are,' he said graciously, handing him the paper.

'It's not mine.'

'Harry said to hand you the paper when it arrived.'

'Why?' asked Ken suspiciously.

Nick began a long tirade of complaint. 'I don't know. How am I supposed to know if you don't? I'm supposed to know everything. What time the painters arrive, what time the paper comes . . . supposed to read people's minds. I haven't had a cup of tea all day.' He walked out in angry dignity whilst Ken said to Doreen:

'Is this to encourage me to apply for a job?'

'No idea.' She obviously wasn't going to divulge anything, particularly as Harry was coming in.

Harry, like Nick, was in a complaining mood. 'Told 'em to take a funny run, idle buggers. Painters and decorators, my back side! Couldn't decorate a bloody cake.'

'It's not easy to decorate a cake,' said Ethel, immediately taking offence, and Harry groaned aloud.

'All right, Ethel. Percy wants another pot of

coffee. Can you fix it? How's the head, Ken?' he asked.

'Coming off,' Ken told him.

'Read the paper yet?'

'No. Harry, I'm going home. I don't want a job. End of conversation. And I tore your cheque up.'

'That's a bit off.' Harry sounded genuinely hurt and Ken felt ashamed.

'I'm sorry. Otherwise I might have cashed it. I'll be in touch. Thanks for last night. At least – most of it.'

'You can't just go. Read the paper!' yelled Harry.

'No,' Ken snapped at him.

'I put an advert in it, Ken. For you.'

'What?' He was completely taken aback.

'I put an advert in. "Ex-fireman seeks . . ." Now where the hell is it?' He scrabbled through the paper. 'You know – "anything suitable considered – anything legal. P.O. Box whatever". Where the bloody hell is it? It's not in! It's not bloody in!'

'You can ring them up and take it out again unless you're the ex-fireman, because I think it's a load of crap. I've a good mind to punch you on the nose, Harry.' Ken made a feeble, threatening gesture, but Harry wasn't listening as he was still scouring the paper.

'I can't believe it. Maybe it's an early edition or—'

In sudden temper Ken lashed out at the newspaper, tearing it in half.

'Hey!' said Harry in indignation. 'Just watch what you're bloody doing.' But he was still trying to scan the paper.

'Are you listening, Harry?' yelled Ken even louder than before. 'You just can't do that.'

With expert timing, 'number eight' put his head round the kitchen door. 'Where's my coffee?'

'I'm really bloody angry about this, Harry,' said Ken, ignoring him.

'I'm sorry, I'm sure.' He looked up from the paper offendedly. He may have been pissed, he thought, but he had gone to considerable trouble. And now the ungrateful sod . . .

'Coffee,' persisted number eight.

'Can you please wait in the dining-room,' said Harry severely.

'I told you I was rushing—'

'As I've said before, the kitchen is for staff only.' He picked up a pot of tepid coffee and practically hurled it at him.

'Thanks,' said number eight, departing in a sulk.

Harry, now as angry as Ken, turned to vent his wrath on him. 'That's it, Ken,' he sneered. 'Hard done by. Had an accident. World against you.'

'Shut it.'

'You don't want helping. You want to have a little wheeze and sit in your bloody field, watching the weeds grow.'

'I'm going to see to my bike.' He would have liked to have seen to Harry, too, but he decided against it at the last moment.

Unaware of his escape from a nasty fate, Harry shouted after him, 'What's wrong with getting a few jobs? You might start paying your way!' But he was already out of earshot.

Just then Doreen came through with the dishes and put them down by the sink. 'What did you say to number eight?' she began. 'He's—'

'Not now, Doreen,' Harry snapped, having worked himself into a toweringly bad mood.

'Sorry I spoke,' she replied, going straight out again and leaving Harry to contemplate the ungratefulness of man.

Ken was in despair as he dismantled bits of bike on the pavement outside the Grand Hotel. He had never felt so humiliated and his fierce pride was deeply wounded. He hardly noticed Doreen standing there with a mug of tea until she cleared her throat impatiently.

'Thought you might want this.'

'Thanks.' He looked up quickly, almost furtively.

'What's up with the bike?'

'Amal carb.'

'Means nothing to me.'

'Well, it's broken,' Ken replied impatiently.

'Are they easy to replace?'

'I'll have a look around.' His voice had a dull, beaten quality. 'Don't make these things any more.'

'Expensive?'

'Not really.'

'So you can afford to fix it?'

'Yeah.'

'Because I could lend you a few pounds if—'

'Listen, I don't know what Harry has said to you—'

'Nothing,' she said quietly.

'I'm not a pauper, all right? Bloody hell!'

'It's not a sin to need some cash.'

'Isn't it?'

'Let me lend you enough to repair your bike?'

'No! You don't know me, Doreen! I wish people would stop . . .' He was quite desperate now. 'I need – it's not just the bike, Doreen, bless you, it's my caravan, and even if I pay for that it doesn't help me finish, or start, my home. It doesn't stock the garden. It's a problem I've got, and I've just got to think my way out of it.'

'Right. And what's wrong with Harry's scheme then? You could at least wait and see what replies you get.'

Ken became almost apoplectic. 'Are you – did he send you to. . . ?'

'You always like this?' she asked in a reasonable voice.

'Yeah.'

'No wonder you're by yourself.'

'That's right. No wonder.'

'Harry really likes you, Ken. He never stops talking about you.'

'Yeah. It's the same for me. I bore my caravan stupid.'

'But he's right. You're as stubborn as—'

'Finished?'

'No.'

'Like this with your husband, were you?'

'That's cheap.'

Instantly Ken regretted what he had said. 'Sorry,' he mumbled inadequately. But it was too late. Doreen had gone.

Ken swore as he crouched down again beside his bike. A few seconds later he had trapped his finger with a spanner and he rose to his feet with a wild cry, leaping around with his hand under his armpit.

Harry was behind the desk looking noble when Ken returned to the reception area of the Grand Hotel.

'Harry?'

But Harry was hurt and continued to look noble.

'I'm sorry.'

'Okay.'

'Not small sorry. Big sorry.'

'I was just trying to help.'

'Look, Harry, I'm an ungrateful bastard. We both know that.'

Harry shrugged. 'A lot's happened since we were in the Brigade. Things have changed. You've got your field; I've got my hotel.'

'Yeah – well, you're not on the edge of losing it, are you?'

'I can't do much for you.'

'You've already done a lot. I just came to say I'm sorry I was so ungrateful.'

'It's your pride,' observed Harry. 'Always been a problem with you. Over the years. You should have married, settled down.'

'Look where –' Ken stopped abruptly.

'Yeah – look where it got me.'

'I didn't mean to say that.'

'It doesn't matter. Okay, it didn't get us very far. But it knocked a few rough corners off. Who do you think you are – the Lone Ranger?'

'I like to be independent.'

'You don't know when to stop.'

'I know, but I am grateful. Can I have another cheque, please? And can I borrow your telephone to ring Mr Fowler?'

Harry instantly thawed and treated him to a hopeful smile. 'You can use the office.'

Before he went, however, Ken was determined to make himself clear. 'I'm going to work for it, though, Harry – the money. As soon as I've fixed the bike, I'll do some painting. I don't want something for nothing.'

Harry raised his eyebrows. 'Of course not,' he replied tactfully, not anxious to start Ken off on another tirade.

'You're a good mate, Harry.'

'I know I am. So what about my idea?'

'Yes.'

'Yes what?'

'Yes, I suppose so. I've got to find the money from somewhere, haven't I? And it wasn't under my pillow this morning, so . . .'

'Smashing.'

'But I tell you one thing, Harry. If we get any replies – nutters apart – I'll eat my helmet. Is Doreen in the office?'

'Expect so.' He paused. 'Going to make your peace?'

Ken grinned. 'Something like that.'

* * *

'Do you accept apologies?'

Doreen looked up from her desk in the office. 'In certain cases.'

'Am I one?'

'You might be.'

'I'm sorry. I was rude. I can be rude.'

'I can be rude too,' she said.

'Am I forgiven? Harry's forgiven me.'

'Harry's a pushover.'

'Yeah.'

'Are you staying?'

'Yeah. I'm painting.'

Suddenly Doreen laughed. 'I'll start defrosting. I might have thawed in a day or so.'

'Thanks.' There was a pause while they looked at each other with sudden understanding. 'Okay,' said Ken, as if she had asked him a question, 'can I use the phone?'

'Do you want me to go out?'

'No, no. I'm just going to buy a little time, if I can.' He dialled a number, waited and then, mustering all his courage, said, 'Mr Fowler? It's Ken Boon here. Afternoon.'

But he received no cheery greeting. 'Well?'

'I'll come straight to the point.'

'Yeah?'

'Got myself a job.'

'Makes a change.'

'I can give you a hundred now. More later.'

'Live now, pay later?'

'Mr Fowler – I'm trying.'

'Yeah. Where's the rest?'

'End of the week.'

'It had better be.'

When Ken had put the phone down Doreen asked, 'Scrape through all right?'

'Just about,' replied Ken.

Chapter Five

Harry descended the steps of the *Evening Mail* offices with an armful of envelopes. He looked confident. But once back at the Grand Hotel his confidence disappeared completely. He sat at the kitchen table with Ken and Doreen. Ethel, busy with her chores, eyed them dourly.

'Double glazing anyone?' said Harry mournfully as he held up a couple of the letters.

Ken smiled grimly as he rifled through his own pile. 'I can have my fortune told for twenty quid. My feet rubbed for fifteen – everything rubbed for fifty.'

'I'm not prepared to stand here and listen to –' began Ethel. Ken, however, was adamant.

'I'm sorry, Ethel, but you want to read some of these. In fact, you don't want to read them.'

'I tell you what I wouldn't do, and that's try and sell double glazing in the Midlands,' commented Doreen as she sighed over her own batch of envelopes.

'Keep all the stamps,' commanded Ethel.

'Yes,' she replied dutifully.

'Some of these haven't been franked,' said Harry.

'Boil the kettle, Ethel,' put in Doreen. 'Harry's steaming stamps.'

Ken put down one of his letters. 'He wants to hear all my sins, and he's enclosed a stamped addressed envelope.'

'Another stamp, see!' said Harry. He turned to Ken. 'Besides, you'd need a parcel, not an envelope for your sins.'

'Thank you, St H.'

'Just like two soft kids,' complained Ethel.

'So far,' said Ken, 'apart from the ones I've taken the trouble to mention, I've had twelve begging letters and assorted requests about my body, my mind and my future life. None of 'em was very practical.'

Harry nodded wisely whilst Doreen said, 'There are so many unfulfilled needs in this world, aren't there?'

'It's the loneliness,' remarked Ethel. 'It gets to them all in the end.' Her voice had a hollow sound.

'They can't take it,' said Ken briskly.

But Harry was keen to pontificate. 'You're too hard, mate. You could start a bureau.'

'What for?'

'Lost souls.'

'Blimey.'

'They'd be queueing up.'

'And what would you expect me to do with them?'

'Listen. And try to give them a little human nourishment.'

'I can't afford to dish out bangers and chips.'

'I'm talking about the spirit,' said Harry pompously while Doreen and Ethel tried hard not to laugh.

Ken however was not amused. Merely impatient. 'I'll leave that to the clergy,' he said.

'Priests are not always what these souls are looking for. They want the man in the street, a companionable chat, a little counselling.'

'Why don't you do that?' asked Doreen innocently, still looking through the correspondence.

'Do what?'

'Be a counsellor.'

'Leave it out!'

Ken and Harry gloomily surveyed the pile of envelopes.

'Nice idea, Harry,' said Ken.

'Yeah.' He sounded very deflated.

'Few more?' Doreen had a determined cheerfulness to her that was almost frightening.

'Come on,' said Harry, getting regretfully to his feet. 'We've got a business to run. Get painting, you,' he said, pointing at Ken.

'Right.'

'Look at this!' Doreen had opened another letter and had found a ten-pound note. She held it aloft like a talisman.

'Ten quid,' said Ken wonderingly, coming over to her, staring at the note.

But Harry was less convinced. 'Ha bloody ha. You just put that in there.'

'I didn't. There's a letter,' she said indignantly.

Harry grabbed the ten-pound note and held it up to the window light whilst Doreen pulled out the letter.

'What's it say?'

'It's real – I think,' muttered Harry.

Doreen unfolded the letter and Harry peered anxiously over her shoulder.

'Headed notepaper. That's not cheap these days.'

'It's from Barney Spitz Promotions.'

'Who?' asked Ken in bewilderment.

'It says, "If you want to collect the other nineteen of these, call me" – signed Barney Spitz Promotions.'

'Nineteen more. That's . . .'

'One hundred and ninety pounds.'

'So two hundred pounds plus my cheque . . .' pronounced Harry.

'I can pay Fowler. Who's Barney Spitz?'

'Ring him and find out. Come on. Use the office phone.' Harry snatched the letter from Doreen and marched Ken out of the kitchen.

'Haven't you forgotten something?' Doreen asked patiently.

'What?' Ken looked back vaguely.

'The ten-pound note,' she said.

Barney Spitz's premises were more like a big cupboard than an office. Every available space – walls, desk, floor – was crammed with posters and photographs of Head for Heights – the band he represented. Demo tapes and a drum kit spilled everywhere and surmounting everything was an enormous poster of James Dean – head down, standing on a street pavement, collar turned up.

When Ken came into the office he stumbled over a box full of copies of Head for Height's first single: 'Inflammatory statements'.

Barney Spitz was a morose man, eating a Big Mac. Ken soon realised that he took himself very seriously.

'You're Ken.'

'That's right.'

'I knew it was you. I'm going to ask you a very strange question, and you shouldn't think it's cranky or anything, although it might . . . In fact, no, I won't ask you now – I'll ask you later. Have you brought your uniform?'

'No. No. I don't have one.'

'What can we do about that, I wonder? 'Scuse me eating.'

'I'm still not quite sure what you want me to do.'

'I'm improvising . . . I've got the start or rather the effect, it's the detail. No, in fact I can be quite specific. I've got the location.'

Ken looked at him, completely mystified. 'For?'

'I can't offer you coffee. We could pop out.'

'No, it's okay.'

'Sit down then. The single's called "Inflammatory Statements", which I think is good – titlewise – although we're going to have to alter the lyrics to fit it slightly . . . But I just can't get any attention for the band, you know. What can you do these days? They're so blasé. You ring up and say you're launching a band.' He shook his head. 'Nothing . . . And the thing is the music is terribly good.'

Ken interrupted him briskly. 'You put ten pounds in a letter to me and said come and collect the rest.'

'I'm thinking "Head for Heights" – that's their name . . .'

'Not "Inflammatory whatsits"?'

'That's the song. No, I'm thinking "Head for Heights" and yes, I'm thinking "Inflammatory Statements" and I'm reading the paper and the press release is Friday, right, so it's urgent. And there you are: ex-fireman. Ken, I want you to climb up a gasometer and hang up our banner.'

There was a brief, poignant silence.

'What gasometer?' Ken said eventually.

'Near Nechells. It's disused.'

'You can't go climbing gasometers for fun. It's dangerous.'

'I can't really go above two. I'll tell you my problem.'

'No, no, really . . . I just—'

Barney began to try and steamroller him. 'No, you see, well okay. First I'll ask you the question, the one I mentioned. Now, don't misunderstand me – if I said are you psychic how would you respond?'

Ken hesitated.

'Of course, I don't like the word,' said Barney hastily. 'I just, anyway I just wanted to ask. No big deal, because you must see the coincidence. I've got this concept and then *pffff*! . . . there's my man advertising in the paper. I've had other experiences . . .' His voice tailed away. Then he seemed to have a sudden idea. 'You don't get crackles or clicks or anything on the phone?'

'I don't think so.'
'Anyway, will you do it?'
'No.'
'Let me play you the track.'
'Look—'
'I'll just play you the track . . .'
Barney put on a cassette of 'Head for Heights' and Ken had to acknowledge that it had quality.
'Why's it called "Inflammatory Remarks" – whatsits?'
'That's my concept. Something slightly dangerous . . . An edge . . . Hence the title. Hence the stunt.'
'Well, good luck.' Ken got up to go.
'I'm desperate for you to do it, Ken, because I had a really good feeling about our meeting. Tomorrow's very important for me.'
'I'm sorry.' He shrugged.
'Two hundred pounds. You can walk away from that, can you?'
'Not easily.'
'I'll tell you. Come. Come tomorrow. If it feels wrong tomorrow, you say no – no quarrel.'
Ken shrugged again.
'Please,' said Barney. He was really pleading and Ken didn't know what to say.
'I'll come and have a look,' he said at last, reluctantly.
Barney's face lit up.
'But the fact that I'm coming doesn't mean I'll do it,' said Ken firmly.

When Ken arrived at the location the next morning, Barney had everything organised. The gasometer, looking appallingly high, a fireman's costume, a banner and the three members of Head for Heights were all present. He had also created a strong atmosphere of expectation.
'No,' said Ken, looking up at the gasometer.

‘Don’t climb all the way up,’ said Barney placatingly. ‘Just enough to get a photograph.’

‘It’s too dangerous and probably illegal. Have you asked anybody?’

Barney ignored him. ‘What are we talking about? A few steps – count the steps – it’s probably a tenner a step. I’ll give you a tenner a step. Okay?’

‘Look, I’d jump at it if I thought it was even half sensible.’

‘Ken, don’t do this. Because I *know*, right? – *know* it’ll be all right.’

Leslie, the singer with Head for Heights, strode up looking impatient. ‘Is he going up or what?’ he rasped.

‘Just relax, Leslie, please.’

‘What’s the problem?’ he persisted. ‘Bit high for you?’ he said directly to Ken.

‘Actually Ken’s an ex-fireman,’ confided Barney.

‘Oh. Why “ex”?’

Before Barney could answer a group of journalists trudged towards them. Barney suddenly became frantic. ‘Ken, please.’ His voice was shrill.

But Ken stolidly pointed at the bottom of the gasometer. ‘Look at that grease. The higher you are, the worse it’ll get. There’ll be no grip. No way.’

‘He’s bottled it,’ said Leslie contemptuously. ‘I’ll do it myself.’

‘Don’t be ridiculous, Les.’ Barney tried to appear calmer. ‘I’ll talk to the papers.’ He turned back to Ken, twitching slightly but with a deadly, almost hypnotic patience. ‘I appreciate your feelings.’

But Leslie was not to be put off. He grabbed the banner and ran towards the gasometer. ‘I’ll do it myself.’

‘Here we go,’ sighed Ken.

‘Leslie, you’re being a complete wally!’ shrilled Barney as Leslie began to climb.

'You'd better stop him,' said Ken.

Meanwhile, instinctively sensing trouble, the press began to move in.

'How can I? They're already here. I mean, I don't want to sound callous, Ken, but this is the stunt, right? Dangerous, yes – but that's the point, isn't it?' His voice rose higher.

'No,' replied Ken quietly.

Barney looked aghast. 'Ken, don't . . . He'll be all right, won't he? He's incredibly talented.'

Ken shook his head and stared up as Barney's incredibly talented singer climbed higher.

'Hey, Spitzy!' cried Leslie, who had now reached halfway up the gasometer. 'How's your windy fireman?'

'Don't be such a prick, Leslie,' yelled Barney. 'Don't mind him, Ken.'

'I don't,' replied Ken.

'Ralph!'

'Yeah?'

'Ralph, come up and hold the flag. I want to do my hair.'

'Leslie, just watch what you're bloody doing,' yelled Barney who was not amused. He then turned round to the eagerly assembled press and gave them an embracing wave of his hand. 'Gentlemen. A good morning. Hi. "Inflammatory Statements". By Head for Heights. I'd introduce the lead, but as you can see he's busy right now.'

'He's being a complete cretin,' said Ralph, beginning to get worried.

'Ralph,' admonished Barney.

'What's the fireman going to do?' asked a reporter curiously.

'This is Ken Boon. He's our safety – he's our stunt . . . consultant. That right, Ken?'

The reporters stood before him, their pencils

poised, whilst the photographers raised their cameras.

'No,' said Ken.

Barney was temporarily saved from further embarrassment by Leslie reaching the top of the gasometer. He stretched across, fastened the banner, looked down and waved vigorously.

'Oi, windy! Look at this! Head for –' But Leslie was over-confident. Suddenly he slipped. He screamed with fright, and his free hand grabbed the banner. To everyone's horror he slithered several yards down it and then came to a halt. swinging and hanging in mid-air. He continued to scream and the sound was wafted down to them harshly, like a wild animal in pain.

'Oh no. Oh Christ!' began Barney, staring up at the swinging Leslie hopelessly.

'Call the fire brigade. Go on!' shouted Ken as he rushed to the bottom of the gasometer.

Barney turned to the third member of the band. 'Jim, there's a box to the right of the gate. Get the fire brigade. Move it.'

Jim sprinted off. Ken had already started the ascent.

As Ken climbed, the memories of his eighteen years in the fire service flooded back to him and he felt the return of the old heady excitement that he had not experienced for months. All he missed was the companionship, the fact that the lads should be down there, cheering him on.

Ken looked up to see Leslie, a speck clinging to the top. He seemed curiously insect-like, almost unimportant. But Ken had been trained to save life, and like any professional rescuer he was single-minded enough to climb on, and on.

Because he was moving slowly, Ken felt no constriction in his chest but he knew if he went too fast he'd be finished – and so would Leslie. There was a slight wind – nothing too fierce – and as soon as he was in earshot Ken began to chat lightly to the swaying boy.

'No problem. Just hang around,' he said, climbing steadily. 'I'll get you down and no hassle.'

'I'm gonna fall.'

'No you're not. You're going to be fine and I'm going to get you down and then we'll all have a cup of tea.'

'It's not so easy.'

'Yes it is. Just try and relax.' A cup of tea. Yes, thought Ken, a cup of tea on his own more like. If he'd been back in the Brigade it would have been different, completely different. A hard slog somewhere and then back to the rest room; a happy crowd of lads, exhausted, noisy, making tea and toast and beans and bangers. Then a game of pool or darts and maybe even a watch of the telly. Together.

Ken climbed on, thinking of his caravan and the bare field and the piles of building materials that his pension couldn't cash-flow him through. It wasn't right.

'Don't look down,' he called up to Leslie. 'Just hold on . . . It'll be all right . . . Just hold on.'

The press responded enthusiastically to the imminent disaster and held their cameras high.

Slowly, wheezing slightly, but well in control of himself, Ken drew parallel with Leslie. He could see the sweat glistening on the boy's brow and his lips moving wordlessly. Was he praying, or what? Ken spoke to him softly and urgently and all his old fire-service adrenalin began to flow.

'Leslie. Listen to me. You'll be all right. I want you to swing, okay? And I'm going to grab you. Just trust me. I'm not going to let you go. Now swing . . .'

'I can't move.'

'You can. Swing.'

'No.'

'If you don't swing, you'll fall.'

Leslie said nothing.

'Do you hear me?'

Still nothing.

'Leslie—'

Silence.

'For God's sake! Don't you understand? If you don't bloody swing, you'll bloody fall.'

Suddenly, desperately, Leslie swung. Ken grabbed and jerked him into the stanchion in front of him and held him there. Below them fire engine sirens were dimly heard. Ken listened to them and sighed. If only he was still with them. He felt a rush of indignation. Here he was, doing his old job, and hardly wheezing. He thought of Ponderosa and sighed again.

As the sirens drew nearer, Barney continued to field the press.

'Front page stuff, Barney,' said Ralph.

'He's twenty-one – with a wonderful voice,' he told the reporters whilst the cameras clicked away.

'Where'd you get the other guy?' asked one reporter.

'Resourcefulness on my part,' said Barney. 'And you can see it's needed. A bit of security – I knew that's what was wanted –' And he proceeded to rattle away whilst Ralph removed himself from the vicinity. He felt like throwing up.

Ken continued to hang on to Leslie who was traumatised.

'Just another few minutes,' said Ken softly.

'We're going to fall,' whimpered Leslie, his whole body rigid. 'We're going to fall.'

'No. We're fine. The brigade will get us down. I liked your song, by the way.'

'What?' He sounded completely uncomprehending.
'I liked your song.'
'Oh shit!' said Leslie.
The sirens were getting closer and Ken looked down. He signed at the wildly gesticulating Barney. 'Looks like your manager's doing well.'
'He's a right wally,' shivered Leslie, closing his eyes. He opened them again and began to whimper, 'We're gonna fall.'
'No we're not. Look – the engine's here and the ladder's going up.'
'I'm slipping.'
'No.' Ken held him tighter. 'You're steady as a rock.'
A few seconds later the top of the ladder hove into view. With his hands over the top rung was John. 'Blimey,' he said, almost frozen with shock. 'What the hell are you doing up here?'
'Just hanging about,' replied Ken.

In the kitchen of the Grand Hotel everyone was gathered around a copy of the *Gazette*. Ken and Leslie adorned the front page, the photograph showing Ken holding a very frightened Leslie.
'Look at you! Handsome sod,' said Harry.
'Local hero,' put in Doreen.
Ethel was determined to savour every word. 'Read it to me, Harry. I haven't got my glasses.'
'No. Ethel, it's a lot of rubbish,' said Ken, embarrassed.
'Listen, mate, if you'd wanted an advert for Box 13 you couldn't have written it better yourself.'
'But I don't.'
'We'll be inundated with offers.'
'It's "we" now, is it?' asked Doreen innocently.
'It was my idea.' Harry was defensive.

'You're welcome to it. Did Fowler call, Doreen?'

'No.'

'Has Spitz paid yet?'

'He couldn't even pay the fine. That little stunt is going to cost him a lot of money.'

'He's got to pay you.'

'Well, he said he would. I think he probably will – eventually. But it's today I need it.'

The telephone rang in the office and Doreen went to answer it, dashing past Nick who was coming in with a large pile of letters.

'I'm going home.' Ken stood up.

'You can't,' said Harry flabbergasted.

'Look, Harry. I said no. No. It was a good laugh, all right? I nearly got myself killed for a nutter. And for nothing. That's it.'

'You're a fool.'

'Yeah, I am. Anyway, thanks for everything. I'll see you. I'll come and sell you a few veggies.'

'Do that,' said Harry. The disappointment was hard-etched in his voice.

Ken walked hurriedly into reception just as Doreen was putting down the phone in the office.

'I'm off.'

'Right.'

'Wasn't Fowler, was it?'

'No.'

'Well . . .'

'What?'

'Nothing.' He fidgeted uncomfortably. 'You'll have to come and look at my field.'

'Right . . . what will you do about the money?'

'No idea. I'll think of something.'

'Let me know what you do.'

'I will.' He grinned and walked away. Doreen wondered if she would ever see him again.

Ken's bike chugged down the country lane leading to Ponderosa. Then, as he drew alongside the field, he gasped and stopped, sitting astride his bike uncomprehendingly. The caravan had gone. There was a hole in his fence and his household effects were strewn about in the open.

For a while he still sat there. Then, with leaden spirits he walked to the telephone box. Anxiously he waited for the ringing tone to be answered. Eventually it was. He pressed in his 10p and said: 'Harry – it's Ken. About those letters?'

'What's up?'

'Fowler's repossessed my caravan.'

'Gawd.'

'So I'll need the ready to get it back. But I s'pose we've run out of envelopes.'

'No.'

'How – the advert only went in that once.' Suddenly a suspicion gripped him. 'Harry—'

'Yeah?' His voice was guilty, very guilty.

'Did you put that advert in again?'

'Well—'

'Harry?'

'Yeah, I did.'

'Why?' Ken's voice was steely.

'You're gonna be out of coins in a minute, my son.'

'I can afford another.'

'That's just a waste of—'

'I said why, Harry.'

There was a vast throat-clearing operation the other end. Then Harry said lugubriously, 'Well, there was no harm in capitalising on your bravery. And besides—'

'Yes?'

'I didn't think you were out of the wood yet.'

'The wood?'

'The financial one. I mean it doesn't make sense

on your pension, does it? Not all that self-sufficiency.'

'It *will* make sense.'

'And meanwhile you've been repossessed. What would you have done without your Uncle Harry?'

'Any more envelopes then?' asked Ken ungraciously.

'Quite a few.'

'And?'

'Couple of old ladies wanted regular shopping done, more double-glazing, a bloke wants to know if you're interested in leather goods and—'

'Sounds great so far, doesn't it? All the same old rubbish.'

'I *said* and—'

'Well?'

The pips began to go and when he dug in his pockets Ken found he hadn't, after all, got any more small change.

'I'll call you back,' he rapped.

'Come home,' yelled Harry. 'All is forgiven.'

Chapter Six

'You'll get your caravan back when you can pay me.' Fowler was in an uncompromising mood as he sat, feet up, behind his desk.

'I've got work now,' said Ken. 'Lots of it.'

'That field?'

'No – ' Ken hesitated.

'Then what?'

'It's – er – consultancy work.' There was a pause and then he added quickly, 'Very rewarding.'

Fowler grinned patronisingly. 'And how would a redundant fireman get consultancy work, eh?'

Ken smarted under his contempt and for a moment contemplated landing him one. He decided against it. 'All right – I'm working in a casino.'

'As a consultant?'

'Not quite.'

'Well, you can't be a bouncer with your lungs. Don't tell me you've got a job as a croupier. You're not really the type.' Fowler folded up with laughter.

'No,' said Ken. 'I'm in a more minor role. But it brings in the loot.' He got to his feet with dignity. 'I want my caravan back,' he said.

'I'll see the colour of your money first,' replied Fowler.

Ken stood in front of the mirror in the men's room of the casino adjusting his bow tie. Pleased with his immaculate dinner-jacket and appearance but depressed by the morning's interview with Fowler, Ken sighed and hurried out. If only – his thoughts returned to the gasometer and his dramatic rescue. If only he could be back in White Watch. But in his heart he knew this could never be.

Standing in the reception area of the casino, Ken went about his task of welcoming guests, opening doors and hovering about in a helpful manner as the mixed clientele arrived and made their way past the desk and the cloakroom to the casino beyond. Occasionally he took someone's coat.

The casino was very up-market but some of its members were definitely not. McGeary, a forty-year-old car dealer walked into the club, chatting loudly with his female companion. He held out his top coat to Ken but this was swiftly followed by his companion's fur coat. Taken by surprise, Ken snatched at the arm of the fur coat and missed. It fell to the floor and McGeary gave him a contemptuous look.

'You're a clumsy lout, aren't you?' he cursed.

'I'm very sorry, sir.'

'So you should be. That coat cost money.' McGeary brushed past him.

Doreen, very smartly dressed in her capacity as trainee croupier, appeared from inside the casino. 'All right?'

'Not so bad,' said Ken, feeling deeply humiliated by the encounter.

'You look all right in a suit.'

'I look like a coat hanger.' He told her about McGeary.

'Take no notice,' she said briskly. 'You'd be surprised who can afford membership.'

'I'm learning.'

'Keep smiling till two-thirty and I'll run you home.'

'Do you mean home?'

'I mean the Grand Hotel. Harry'll be waiting up for you.'

'I'm a big boy now. I've got my own key. And by the way—'

'Yes?'

'Thanks for getting me this job.'

'You being funny?'

'No – I mean it.'

She smiled. 'It's only temporary.'

'Yeah.'

'Till you get on your feet – and a few more envelopes come in with something—'

'Suitable? That'll be the day.'

A couple came up and Ken burst into ingratiating speech. 'Good evening, sir, madam. Can I take your coats?' He took them with a flourish for Doreen's benefit.

'Very impressive,' she said, smiling at him.

'Thank you, madam,' he replied.

A small writing lamp illuminated the empty reception desk of the Grand Hotel. The remaining area was quite dark, except for the street lights which picked out some of the floor. But after a few moments the lighted area of the hall floor was obscured by a lengthening shadow, and a figure appeared, trying the locked entrance doors. After a few abortive attempts, the figure fumbled for a coin and began to tap loudly on the glass.

When the figure had been tapping, increasingly loudly, for about five minutes, the slow-moving figure of Nick appeared at the top of the stairs. He was wearing pyjamas and was intent upon the task of getting his arm into his dressing gown and not losing one of his slippers.

Standing in the porch and making all the noise was Frank Warren, He was slightly built, Irish, good-looking, but very much the worse for wear. Looking generally ruffled, he wore a dirty, torn mac and was clearly in considerable distress.

'Is that you, Ken?' grumbled Nick. Then he saw that it wasn't. 'Who are you?'

Frank mouthed a reply to which Nick merely muttered, 'What?'

He had now reached the bottom of the stairs and was waving at Warren to keep quiet. The noise abated for a moment and Nick walked behind the desk and began to poke about. Then the tapping began again and Nick stood up angrily, holding the hotel register he had been looking at. The hasty action dislodged the small light which fell to the ground and smashed with a loud noise.

'Buggeration! Now look what you made me do! I'm not having this – just clear off – ' He made dismissive gestures at the door.

Harry suddenly emerged at the top of the stairs, awoken by the commotion Nick was making. He took up a threatening stance, wondering if the hotel was being attacked. But his clothing – a T-shirt and a bathrobe – reduced him to an almost ludicrous figure.

'Nick?'

'Eh?'

'What's going on?'

'*I* don't know! Some mental case outside. I haven't even got my teeth in.'

Frank Warren was now gazing at the pair of them through the glass.

Harry groaned. 'I'll look after it.' He switched on the main lights from behind the desk as Nick slowly ascended the stairs, grumbling loudly to himself.

'What is it you want, mate?' said Harry through the closed door. 'We're closed.'

Frank pushed a fiver through the letterbox. Harry picked it up and held it up to the door in surprise.

'What's this for then?'

Another note came through the letterbox, and

then a third. Hurriedly, Harry unlocked the door before the crouching figure could insert a fourth.

'Is this a hotel?'

'Just about.'

'Let me in then, eh?'

'Hang on,' replied Harry dubiously, blocking the entrance. But Frank was desperate.

'Don't say you're full . . . Come on . . . I'm done in.'

'Everything all right, Harry?' asked Nick from his vantage point on the stairs.

'Is it the money? I've got more if that's the problem.' His desperation was increasing.

'Everything's fine, Nick,' said Harry. He added rather grudgingly to Frank, 'You'd better come in.'

He unlocked the door and the dishevelled figure stumbled in. 'You're a friend. How much have I given you so far?'

'Plenty. Watch out for the broken glass. The night porter had the light over.'

'Just point me towards a bed.'

'I have to sign you in first.'

'Tomorrow,' said Frank firmly.

'What's your name?'

Frank was suddenly confused, hesitant, and Harry looked at him suspiciously. 'You're in a right old state. What's happened?'

Frank replied obliquely, 'P. Brandon.'

'What's that now?'

'P. Brandon.'

'Is that your name?'

'That's right.'

'You're in room number five, Mr Brandon. Top of the stairs, and breakfast is six till nine-thirty.'

'Tremendous.' He hesitated on the stair, anxiously grateful.

'I owe you some change.'

'Keep it. You're a good man.'

‘It’ll pay for the light then.’

‘Whatever you like.’ He turned and Harry watched him limp up the stairs. Should he have let him in? he wondered. Would he murder everyone in their beds before the night was out. It was not a pleasant prospect.

Meanwhile, at the casino, Ken was out of his smart uniform and back in his own clothes. He stood chatting with the assistant manager, a friendly man called Alf, who was paying out his wages.

‘You must miss the old life,’ Alf said. ‘My brother-in-law was in the Brigade. He loved it. It’s special like – almost a club. I mean – don’t you have your secret initiation rights and all that?’

Ken laughed. ‘Not exactly.’

‘So I hear you’re going it alone. Bit of self-sufficiency and all that.’

‘If I can get it – cash-flow problems.’

‘Ah.’

‘So I have to fill in.’

Ken paused while Alf looked at him shrewdly. ‘Bit of an idealist, are we?’

‘I wouldn’t say that.’ Ken was instantly defensive.

‘Why not?’

‘Sounds as if I’ll never make it.’

‘You will – if you persist. I had the chances – went to Australia and all. Now I’ve got this job.’

‘It’s not bad.’

‘Not good enough. I had me own casino out there.’

‘What happened?’

‘Went bust. Like me cinema went bust. And before that me garage.’

‘Blimey.’

‘But I’m persistent. I rebuild. So you ain’t seen nothing yet.’

‘No,’ said Ken, ‘I obviously haven’t.’

'I picks myself up,' said Alf, 'dusts myself down – and starts all over again.'

'Yeah.'

'So you get your cash-flow money, lad, and get stuck into that field. There's nothing like working for yourself. Nothing in the world.'

'That's true,' Ken agreed fervently.

'And you deserve that freedom – everyone deserves it. But you know why most of 'em don't get it?'

'No – why?'

'Because they haven't got the guts,' said Alf. 'Now, there you go, Ken. That should see you all right.'

'Thanks.'

As he pocketed his money, Doreen came in with her coat on. 'And I should thank you too.'

'I thought it would make a change from shifting furniture at the Grand.'

'You're not kidding.'

'I'll say goodnight,' said Alf. 'I'll see you tomorrow, Doreen.'

'No you won't. It's my night off.'

'Oh yeah.' Alf looked disappointed. Then he turned back to Ken. 'I'll see you, and let me tell you, you've done a damn good job. It's not easy.'

'You can say that again,' said Ken, remembering the humiliating experience of the fur coat.

Doreen fished around in her bag to retrieve her car keys. 'Okay?'

'Yeah.'

'Are we off then?'

'Will you celebrate with me?'

'Celebrate what?' She looked surprised.

'Getting my caravan back!' He patted his wallet. 'Getting my land back. I feel terrific.'

'But it's nearly three in the morning.'

'If you drove slowly we could have breakfast.'

She shook her head.

'What about tonight? I'll buy you dinner.'

'I don't know. Besides, I'd be eating your caravan.'

'I've got enough for both.'

'We'll go halves.'

'No. I don't like that.'

'Suit yourself.'

'Sixty:forty?'

Doreen moved away.

'Fifty-five:forty-five?' He walked after her. 'Fifty-one:forty-nine?'

Finally she turned back to him and grinned. 'It's a date.'

Ken was happy when he arrived back at the Grand. Indeed, all his problems seemed to be dissolving.

Harry sat up yawning as Ken came whistling in. 'Bloody hell, the dawn chorus . . .'

'You didn't have to wait up for me, mum!'

'I wasn't waiting for you,' Harry said indignantly. 'I'm running a twenty-four hour business. Trade's passing at all hours. Just booked one in next to you. Paid cash.'

'So did the casino. I'll be off your hands soon, Harry. I reckon I've got enough to keep Fowler happy now. I'll get my van back and I'm in business. Then it's hallo again Market Gardening and goodbye Box Thirteen.'

'Can't wait to give it up, can you?' replied Harry, disappointed.

'I can't. I want to get out to my place and dig a bit of ground, do something for myself. Don't want to be an errand boy all my life, do I?' Ken paused by the stairs. 'By the way, Doreen sends her love.' He went up to bed, whistling, leaving Harry looking rather sourly after him.

Ken's whistling woke Frank in room number five. He found himself fully clothed between the sheets – and on top of them a very large number of scattered five-pound notes. Sitting up he saw more money on the floor. It was as if it was growing there. Hurriedly Frank leant painfully over the bed, gathered the money up, stuffed it under the pillow and lay back on the bed frowning. What the hell was he to do now?

Feeling quite belligerent, Ken arrived on Fowler's site where two businesses seemed to flourish together – building materials and caravan sales. He found Fowler in his office, looking as if he had been there for some hours and, judging by the stacks of paperwork, would be there many hours yet.

'Mr Boon,' he said, looking up rather wearily. 'All right, are we?'

'Bearing up.'

'That's what I like to hear.'

'I want my caravan back,' Ken stated baldly.

The wary note in Fowler's voice seemed to grow. 'We've already had this discussion, Mr Boon. It *was* your caravan – *now* it's mine.'

'This is what I owed you and the next instalment.' He dumped the money down on the table.

'I see.' Fowler looked at the pile uncompromisingly.

'It's all there.'

'I'm sure it is. Unfortunately your caravan isn't.'

'Come again?'

'I've sold it.'

Ken looked at him unbelievingly. 'What do you mean you've sold it!' His anger grew. 'That was my van!'

'Cash-flow. You signed an agreement. You broke it. I gave you leeway.' He shrugged. 'No joy. I'm sorry. I have to say I'm out of pocket.'

'You're out of pocket! I'd paid you good money! I want my van back, mate.'

Fowler smiled blandly at him. 'I'm a businessman, Mr Boon. Not a magician. It's gone. Now, if you're interested in something more realistic, your money will go a long way towards securing you a very nice used model. Let's go and have a look at what we've got in the yard, shall we? I'm prepared to give you a special price in view of what's happened.'

'I bet you are!' He followed him out, conscious of being done. But what could he do about it?

That morning a disgruntled Ken was back in the Grand Hotel taking a cup of tea to Harry's office. He looked up, preoccupied by the VAT forms in front of him.

'I asked Nick.'

'I don't mind.'

'Lazy beggar. Thanks.'

'Need a hand?'

'Not really – they're my baby.'

'What you up to?'

But Harry was trying to punch the buttons on his calculator and he looked up irritated by the interruption. 'Do you mind?'

'Sorry.'

Harry put the calculator down reluctantly. 'You're not still in the dumps?'

'No.'

'Good.'

'I'm still angry.'

'I said, Ken, you can stay here until you're back on an even keel.'

'I am on an even keel. I want to get going.'

'Then get another caravan. Take Fowler up on his offer.'

'Some offer! I couldn't afford anything he had.'

'Look, Ken, I'm finding this out. Business – you've got to be tough, you've got to drive a bargain. You want to see my bills. It's horrible.'

'What can I do, Harry? I've got a field full of bits and pieces.'

'I'm glad you realise that at last.'

'I'm not daft.'

'Look, mate, cut your losses, go back to Fowler, get him to take back the building materials and swap them for a first-class van with all the trimmings.'

'I can't do that! I'll be back to square one. Worse. I'll never catch up. I could kick myself. I could kick Fowler. I can't Harry. I'd never catch up.'

'That's how it seemed to me, mate, but I persevered. You want to think about it, Ken, really.'

'I have thought about it.'

'You see, I think you're underestimating Box Thirteen. That's done you proud already.'

'Oh yeah? Could have cleared a dozen houses, looked after some teenage psychopaths, and done an old lady's shopping. And you should see today's pickings. There's nothing! There's a few perverts and that bloody double glazing firm. I tell you what I might do and that's go and smash a few windows. That's what I feel like.'

'You want to go back to bed if you ask me.'

'I might at that.'

Nick came in, his sour mood matching theirs. 'Harry, we don't serve breakfast after nine-thirty, do we?'

'What? Don't just barge in, Nick.'

'It's hard to barge through an open door.'

'Yeah, okay. What's this about breakfast?'

'Well, I woke up that mental case in number five and he wants breakfast.'

'He's missed it.'

'He gave me a fiver.'

'A fiver? Well, that's fair dues.'

'Is it? He wants to stay in bed – says he's got a bad leg.'

'He has got a bad leg.'

'I know – that's what I said. My legs aren't great either, if we're discussing legs.' He sounded quite enthusiastic for a change.

'It's all right, Nick. I'm going to see Ethel about some food. I'll get him something.' Ken was anxious to be helpful.

'Thanks, Ken – and keep your pecker up. Something will happen.'

'It had better,' replied Ken abruptly.

But Ken's job was not only to take in Frank's breakfast – it also involved him in taking a look at his ankle.

'Well, I suppose you could call me a paramedic. We did all sorts in the fire brigade.' Ken taped up his ankle while Frank winced.

'Miss it, do you?'

'Well, I've got a bit of a side line at the moment. I help people out. I do anything really. Climbing gasometers, moving furniture. That sort of thing . . . trying to make a few bob . . . I think you ought to get this X-rayed. How did it happen?'

'Do you think it's serious?'

'Could be.'

'To tell you the truth, mister, I'm in dire straits, if you get my meaning.'

'Sorry to hear it. I'm not full of sunshine myself.'

'It's the world,' said Frank wisely.

'Yeah. Expect so.' He didn't sound very encouraging.

'This help business of yours. You get all sorts of jobs, then?'

'It's not so much a business as a between business.'

'Understand. Understand completely. But say I

wanted you to find out a few things for me, could you do that?'

'Are you in trouble with the police?' asked Ken suspiciously.

'Oh no.' He paused. 'No. I tell you what it is. I've given my head a whack and now I'm having a terrible time with the old memory box.' He stared up at Ken hopelessly. 'It's gone.'

'I see,' said Ken sceptically. Then with a little more sympathy he said, 'What are you really saying? You can't remember anything?'

'Not a dicky-bird.'

'What about your name? Your address?'

'Brandon. My name's P. Brandon. That's all I know.'

'P for . . .'

'Haven't a clue.'

'Patrick?'

Frank stared at him miserably. 'You don't believe me, do you?'

'No,' said Ken frankly.

'You want to try it! Waking up in a hotel bedroom knowing nothing except your leg is killing you and your head has blown a fuse.'

'Well, if you're really not bullshitting, ring the police station and they'll sort you out.'

'I can't do that, can I?'

'Why not?'

Instantly he became guarded and Ken's suspicions deepened. 'Because . . . because . . . Look at me . . . I look suspicious, don't I? How did I hurt my leg? And what's more – to tell you the truth I've got a little bit of cash on me.'

'And that's a problem?' Ken's tone was ironic.

'Bit of one. And I've got the fear of God up me.'

'I'm sorry, but I don't see how I can help you,' said Ken brusquely.

'You could find out who I am.'

'How?'

'I don't know.'

'Well, I don't know either. No. Best thing for you, mate, is to rest up, get that leg mended and relax. It'll all come back to you then.'

But Frank suddenly became insistent. 'Let me give you some cash.'

'I'll think about it and get back to you.' But there was no conviction in his voice.

'You're a friend.'

'I haven't said anything yet.'

'But I can see you're a good man.' He winced again. 'If I weren't in so much pain . . .' Frank slumped back against the bed and a number of fivers fluttered to the floor. Ken watched them with interest.

'See you,' he said, walking out and Frank scrabbled to rescue the notes.

'If you wanted to find out where somebody lived but you didn't have their address, what would you do, Harry?'

Harry was busy dealing with a guest at reception and was not pleased at being interrupted. 'Look in the phone book.'

'That's what I thought. Got the phone book, Harry?'

'Excuse me,' he said to his guest, and with heavy patience began to search for the directory. 'What's this for then?'

'I've got a job.'

'What job?' He handed Ken the directory.

'Box Thirteen. Private Investigator,' he said as he walked away.

Harry turned back to his now impatient guest with an apology, but a few minutes later Ken wandered back with the directory just as Harry's guest departed.

'Are we allowed to know what you're investigating?'

'I'm trying to find out who our friend in number five is.'

'Why? Won't he tell you?'

'He doesn't know.'

'Well, his name's in the register.'

'P. Brandon.'

'That's right.'

'He says he's lost his memory.'

'Very fishy if you ask me. Too many five-pound notes by half and he's not budged from that room for a second.'

'He's got a bad leg.'

'I've got a bad back! You've got dodgy lungs. But we still hobble about. I don't think he's lost his memory. I think he's got a few things to forget.'

'That's what I thought.'

'Leave it alone, Ken.'

'Yeah, well . . .'

'That means no, bloody smokie.'

'This is a Box Thirteen job, Harry, and a man with a lot of five-pound notes.'

'Now that's true. I see. How much is Mr Mystery paying you?'

Ken shrugged.

'Oh. I'll tell you what you should do, Ken Boon, and that's stop mucking about and ring Mr Fowler.'

'Listen, I had this great idea about friend Fowler. You're right. I think I should give the materials back.'

'That's right, Ken.'

'Yeah. I thought I'd hire a tipper truck and drive it straight into his office and unload.'

Harry laughed. 'You've always been an obstinate sod.'

'That's right. Now then . . .' He walked away from an exasperated Harry. 'Brandon P., Brandon P. E., Brandon P. W.' Ken returned to the desk and tore a page out of the telephone directory.

'Here! Hang on!'

'It's all right,' he said. 'I'll put it back.'

Ken's desire to find out who P. Brandon was had now become something of an obsession. It was the first time he had been really stretched since he had left the Brigade and there was only the odd incident of the gasometer to remind him that Box Thirteen would ever produce anything of interest. A long line of old ladies' shopping expeditions and double glazing sales tactics stretched across his mind as Ken rode out on his quest.

He had not gone far on his motor bike when he passed a mangled Cortina being extricated from a lamp post by a breakdown crew. He slowed down to scrutinise it closely but the wreck offered no clue. Then he approached the first of the Brandons he had looked up in the directory – a greengrocer's shop. Ken parked the bike, dismounted and went thoughtfully in.

'Next,' said the young woman behind the counter. She had an apathetic yet slightly aggressive air.

'Mr Brandon about?'

'No, he's not. Why?'

'You Mrs Brandon?'

'No. D'you want anything?'

'An apple please. That one. It says P. Brandon on the outside,' said Ken gesturing feebly.

'It says "chemist" next door, but they're not called Mr and Mrs Chemist.' She handed him an apple and someone in the queue behind Ken sniggered.

'Thanks for your help,' said Ken, irritated, and the young woman suddenly relented.

'Brandon died two years ago,' she informed him. 'That'll be 15p.'

Ken paid up and walked out. His task, he knew, was not going to be an easy one.

Outside the shop, Ken stared down at his apple. It didn't look particularly appetising and when he took a bite out of it he found a maggot inside. He crossed the name off his list, swore and got back on his bike. Somehow, all his interest in being a private eye had rather worn off.

His next stop was at a terraced house. It was a dull, overcast morning and the street looked particularly unwelcoming. He knocked and a young woman in a dressing gown answered the door.

'Mrs Brandon?'

'Speaking.'

'I'm not bothering you, am I?'

'As a matter of fact I was in the bath.'

'Is your husband in?'

'You're from the Social, aren't you?'

'No. No, nothing like that.'

'I know I'm being followed about and I don't like it,' she snapped.

'It's not me. I came about your husband, about what happened to him.'

The woman gave Ken a questioning, knowing glance. 'Just got out, have you?'

'Eh?'

'I'm going to visit, but it's such a bloody awful journey to the Isle of Wight.' She sounded guilty.

'No, you see I just wondered if you might have missed him recently?'

'Course I'm missing him. What do you think?'

Just then the woman's Neanderthal boy-friend appeared on the step. He was also clad in a dressing gown. 'What's up, Myra?'

'Says he's a friend of Phil's.'

'So am I, mate.'

'Right.' Ken turned suddenly very friendly. 'All right?'

The boy-friend nodded ponderously. His huge arms hanging loosely at his sides. 'Yeah. Well come back in twenty years and you'll be in time for Phil's reunion party.'

'Yeah?'

'In the meantime, bugger off.' He advanced a couple of threatening steps.

Ken retreated. 'I'm just off.' Then he said from a safe distance, 'Bye now. I'll tell Phil you're both keeping very clean.'

As Ken started up his bike the boy-friend called out something he couldn't hear.

Ken's next port of call was rather more salubrious as he found himself spluttering down a well-to-do street with semis on each side. He checked the numbers, found the right one and slowed to a halt outside it. He turned the engine off, lifted his goggles and was about to dismount when he saw a large 'For Sale' sign stuck across the gate bearing a housing agent's name. Ken hesitated, got off his bike and put it up on its stand.

'Third time lucky,' he muttered.

The house, although obviously expensive, had a slightly sinister, desolate air about it. Ken walked slowly into the garden and carefully closed the gate behind him. He walked up the path to the door and pushed the bell, but there was no ringing noise. Cupping his hands, he looked into the front bay window. There were no curtains and all the furniture was covered by dust sheets. He also noticed that the phone on the floor near the door had its receiver off the hook. Ken strolled round the side of the house towards a high fence and door which separated the front from the back garden. He opened the door and stopped and looked at the freshly turned earth in the bare garden and frowned. What the hell had been going on? The sight of the new earth made him shudder.

He slowly walked through into the back garden and began to examine the freshly dug border. There were no plants – just great piles of earth. Arriving at the kitchen door he found it unlocked. He turned the handle and looked inside. Behind him an unexpected figure suddenly loomed with a raised shovel, but Ken, unaware that he had such a sinister and menacing company, tiptoed into the kitchen.

With the shovel-swinging figure still behind him, Ken went over to the stove and, sleuth-like, tested the kettle for warmth.

'Just what do you think you're doing?'

With a wild cry Ken nearly jumped out of his skin. He swung round, knocking the kettle off the stove. He saw before him an attractive but extremely harassed young woman, dressed in gardening gear with a raised spade in her hands.

'Bloody hell! Be careful, can't you?'

'What d'you mean "careful"? You're snooping in my kitchen.'

Ken partially recovered from the shock. 'I'm really sorry . . . I did try the front door first.'

'Pick up the kettle,' she said, her shovel still at the ready.

Ken cautiously picked it up. 'And the back door was open . . .'

'All right. If you're here about the house, it's sold. Didn't you see the sign? It's ridiculous the Agents haven't moved it. Peter's furious about it. So am I.' She was calming down – just a little.

Ken reacted optimistically to the mention of her husband's name. 'You must be Mrs Brandon.'

‘Of course I’m Mrs Brandon.’ She looked at him as if he was crazy and fingered the handle of the shovel.

‘Terrific!’ He went up to her and held out his hand.

She dropped the shovel, slightly reassured yet completely mystified. ‘How d’you do.’

‘Actually, it’s not about the house, really. It’s about – I mean – is Peter around?’

‘You’re joking. I never see him these days. I get instructions. Today, it’s dig up the border shrubs.’

‘What? Taking them with you?’

‘Oh yes.’

‘Can’t beat a nice japonica,’ said Ken appreciatively.

‘Is Peter expecting you?’

‘Well I had hoped I might find him.’

‘Join the club.’ Her tone was cynical.

‘He’s not gone missing, has he?’ Ken’s former excitement returned and he thought, this detective business – it’s got its points.

‘Just a joke – not a very funny one. It’s only that I’m having to do all this myself.’

‘Maybe I could give you a hand. I’m quite green-fingered.’

‘What were you wanting to see Peter about?’ The suspicion was back in her voice again. No wonder, thought Ken. Attractive young housewife meets intruder.

‘Social call, nothing much. Before you move – ’ He tried to sound very casual.

‘’Cos he didn’t mention anything this morning about anyone popping round.’

‘This morning?’ Ken was suddenly deflated.

‘Yes.’ Mrs Brandon looked at him intently.

‘Well. I’ll . . .’ He moved a couple of paces towards her, trying to get by, knowing he was, after all, at the wrong place.

'Actually, I wouldn't say no to a hand bringing in those plants. My back's like iron . . .'

'Right,' said Ken, anxious not to get marooned.

Mrs Brandon seemed to warm to him. 'And there's a packing case blocking the bedroom door upstairs and I can't move it and it would be really marvellous if you could just . . .'

'Upstairs,' Ken said dubiously.

'I can't tell you, I'm fagged out. You know what Peter's like. He wants every damn thing doing, just so, but he's always too busy himself. Typical.'

'Same old Pete,' said Ken feebly.

'Listen, I'll put the kettle on while you're bringing the rest of the shrubs in, and I've got a nice bit of quiche. Any use?'

'No, I'm having to be careful with . . .' He paused and pointed at his stomach.

'You sure? See how you feel later on. Do you want to borrow Peter's wellies?'

'Uh . . . Well, I could do.'

'Let me see, I saw them just now . . . They're in the . . .'

Behind her Ken could see a figure through the glass front door. 'Look, it's no bother if you . . .' He felt a sense of rising panic as the key turned in the lock and the door opened.

Mrs Brandon turned round and exclaimed, 'Wonders will never cease!'

Ken looked at her in horror. This was obviously Peter Brandon. Now what the hell was going to happen?

'How come you're home?'

'Hallo!' said Brandon in a friendly, disarming way to Ken.

Taken completely by surprise he went on the defensive. 'Now then.'

'How are you? I'm sorry I'm late.' He was so strangely familiar, so friendly.

'So you were expecting . . .' She turned to Ken. 'He was expecting you.'

'Of course.'

'You could tell me, Peter. Honestly, I nearly chucked him out – clunked him with a shovel!'

'Sorry darling. Listen, be a love, go through to the car will you and fetch my briefcase, eh? Be an angel.' He gave her a sugary smile.

'See what I mean,' she said to Ken.

'What's this?' asked Peter nervously. 'What do you mean?'

'I was just telling him all about you, and the way you treat me,' said Mrs Brandon in a light voice.

Peter anxiously cleared his throat as she made her exit. He was more than a rep, thought Ken, more like an area sales manager. Mid-thirties with the suit to match.

'Now listen, what've you said? What did she just say?' He was edgy now.

'No, we were just . . .' began Ken, but Brandon wouldn't let him finish.

'It's all over with Sue. I've told them! It's been finished for weeks, months. Honest to God! You can see for yourself. We're moving for Chrissake. You can't say fairer than that, can you? In a couple of days you'd never know I existed.'

'I think we're at cross purposes, Mr Brandon, you see . . .'

'Don't think you can threaten me!' he began again. 'I've got friends as well, you know, and you know what I'm talking about! So just sod off!'

'That's a bit much. I was just trying to explain what—'

Peter's aggression intensified in the face of Ken's mild behaviour. 'Coming here, worrying my wife. If you've told her, I'll—'

Mrs Brandon suddenly returned with the briefcase and her husband broke off abruptly.

'One briefcase, your highness.'

'You're a complete angel, sweetheart, popsie.' Ken looked at him in disgust. He felt like throwing up.

'I know. I suppose you want tea now? I'm just making some for—'

But Peter, with desperate initiative, was shaking Ken's hand vigorously. 'Actually Brian's got to go.'

'Oh?'

'Sorry.'

'But it's been great seeing you again, kid. Take good care. And don't forget your old mate – and the good old times.'

'Right,' said Ken, half-heartedly entering into the spirit of things.

'Well, nice to have met you, Brian.' She gave him a charming smile. 'Sorry about the mix-up.'

'Think nothing of it,' he replied as he stumbled out.

Chapter Seven

'How's Sherlock Holmes?' asked Harry when Ken had returned to the Grand.

'Terrible.'

'Who is he then? Your friend in number five?'

'I don't know, but he's not in the phone book.'

'I bet he's not. I wish he wasn't in my hotel either. I tell you – the first thing you can find for him is somewhere else to live.'

'What do you mean – *me* find for him?'

'He's your client.'

'No, he's not.'

'You could ask forty pounds a day as a private detective. I rang round. Plus expenses. That's a lot of money.'

'Yeah. Probably a lot of stolen money.'

'That's not your problem.'

'Nor's he, Harry. I'm not interested.'

'You make me laugh. One minute you complain about no money, the next minute you're turning down ready cash.' He was impatient now.

'That's right. One minute you're telling me I'm a fool to take this job, the next minute I'm a fool to turn it down.'

'Well, I'm contradicting myself.' Harry half-laughed.

'I'll see you later,' said Ken, clapping Harry on the back. They might be exasperated with each other, but they were now close enough to remain friends.

'Yeah. Ethel's making a vegetable lasagne tonight.' He raised his eyebrows.

'And I'm missing it.'

'Why?'

'Doreen and me, we're having a little meal. Out.'

Harry grinned. 'Listen to this! Little meal! Sly bugger.'

'What do you mean?' said Ken innocently.

'I thought Doreen was locked and she'd forgotten the combination.'

'It's nothing like that, Harry. It's a celebration – was meant to be a celebration – for getting my van back.'

'And now what's it going to be?'

'Well . . . a commiseration, I suppose.'

'I wish you'd let me speak to this Fowler. I know how to deal with his sort.'

'Okay.'

'Okay what?'

'Okay, speak to Fowler.'

Harry looked amazed. 'What's changed your mind all of a sudden?'

'Nothing. Just that I know when you meet him you'll want to run him over as well.'

Ethel suddenly arrived with tomorrow's menu and showed it to Ken.

'Ken's turning his back on your vegetable lasagne, Ethel.'

'Is he?'

'He's got a date.'

'That's nice. I'll keep some for your lunch then, Ken.'

'Don't worry about me, Ethel.'

'You could always bring her here for supper, couldn't he, Harry?'

'Smashing idea,' said Harry gleefully.

'We've booked a table now,' said Ken with mock regret as he headed up the stairs.

Just as he disappeared out of sight Nick wandered vaguely into reception.

'Nick, are you busy?' Harry asked him.

'I'm getting my allergy back from scrubbing those bathroom tiles. Look!' He threw up his hands which appeared to be completely healthy.

'Can you come and sulk behind reception while I go to the bank?'

'You'd sulk if you had an allergy.'

'Never mind. Ethel's making vegetable lasagne tonight.'

Nick cheered up immediately. 'Lasagne? I love a drop of lasagne. I like a nice carbonara and all.'

'Play your cards right and next week I might even run to gnocchi,' said Ethel.

'Gnocchi! With fine herbs!' Nick was even more pleased and Harry, realising he was completely out-manoeuvred, could only mutter:

'Smashing.'

Frank sat up in bed with a start as Ken knocked.

'Come in.'

'Well, I'll tell you who you're not and that's P. Brandon,' said Ken, coming straight to the point.

'How do you know?'

'Because I looked. I found three in the phone book and unless you're dead or escaped from Parkhurst we're up a blind alley.' Ken passed him the list.

'What about the third?'

'P. Brandon three is a nutter who calls everyone Brian and thought I was from the Mafia. You're better off not being him.'

'I see. Well thanks for trying anyway.'

'It's OK,' said Ken with a shrug.

'So what's next?'

'What's next is nothing, mate.' He was irritated by Frank's complacency.

'Please, Ken, you've got to help me. I'm lying here frantic.' Suddenly he was desperate. 'I'll give you anything you want. And I can start off by paying you for this morning. Hang on.'

'I don't want payment because I don't want the job. Besides, there's nothing more I can do.'

'But look – say I'm not in the phone book, eh? Say I don't live in the area, eh?'

'Say you're not P. Brandon?'

'Yeah.' He paused bleakly and then added with real feeling, 'But if I'm not P.Brandon, Ken, who am I? And where has all this come from?' He lifted up his pillow to reveal all his neat little piles of fivers. There were so many of them that Ken gasped out loud.

'Blimey.'

'See what I mean?'

'Oh yes, I see what you mean all right.'

Ken was silent for some minutes.

'What we have to do is to talk,' he said at last.

'Talk?'

'I have to help you remember. Somehow. Do you remember having a bang on the head?'

'Now why would I remember that?'

'Well, that's what must have started it,' said Ken impatiently. 'Do you think you were in a car crash?'

'I dunno.'

'You've nothing in your pockets?'

Frank gave him a pitying look. 'I checked that out when I recovered consciousness. Nowt.'

'No laundry marks?'

'What?' Frank looked incredulous. 'That's what they say in thirties detective stories. You can't have said that!'

'I did. We must check everything.'

'What about your little grey cells?'

'I beg your pardon?'

'Little grey cells. Hercule Poirot was always worrying at them.'

'Poiret? Now you've remembered someone else? Are you – what did you say – Herculo Poiret?'

'Hercule Poirot. Agatha Christie's Belgian detective.'

'Agatha who?' Ken was now completely at sea.

'Never mind – she's a writer,' said Frank quickly.

Ken looked at him very suspiciously. 'Now if you can remember all that shit, why can't you remember who you are?'

'I don't know. You don't believe me , do you?'

'I don't know what to think. Harry wants you out – that I do know.'

'He doesn't believe me.'

'Harry reckons you're trouble.'

'How can I be – lying here?'

'Potential trouble.'

Frank riffled through his fivers. 'Maybe I am. But I want to know how I got these.'

'Trouble?'

'Mm. Could be I nicked 'em. But I don't think so.'

'Why?'

'I don't feel like a crook. Do I look like one?'

'No one looks like a thief,' said Ken, feeling frustrated. He was getting nowhere.

'I said feels. I'd say if I was.'

'I bet you would.' Ken thought for a moment and then said, 'Let's try a bit of word association.'

'Eh?'

'For someone who reads Agatha wotsit you're very thick. Now let's try it. I'll say home.'

Frank was silent.

'Home,' Ken repeated irritably.

'Yes?'

'Say which word you associate with it,' yelled Ken.

'Sausage.'

'I see. Well, let's keep trying. It might trigger something off. Wife.'

'Unfair.'
'Children.'
'Hospital.'
'Friends.'
'Pub.'
'Any particular pub?'
'Just – pub.' Frank's face was screwed up with effort.
'Okay. Let's carry on. Job.'
'Escape.'
'Money.'
'Bank.'
'Steal.'
'Prison.'
'Home.'
'P. Brandon.'
'Ah. Now, why did you say that?'
'Do you know – I haven't the faintest idea.'
Ken groaned. 'We're back to square one.'
'Tell you what,' said Frank. 'Do you reckon those fivers are marked?'
'Blimey! I didn't think of that. And if they are, I'm not trying to pass any.' He thought for a minute. 'Harry though. I've already paid him.'
Ken shrugged. 'We'll just have to wait until you get your memory back, won't we?' he snapped.
'You don't know what it's like,' wailed Frank. 'I'll tell you – it's bloody awful. I could be anyone.'
For the first time Ken felt really sorry for him.

Sitting behind reception, Nick was reading a lurid gangster paperback when a young policeman entered the foyer of the Grand Hotel and stood just inside the doorway.
'Afternoon.'
'How do?' Nick looked up unwillingly.
'Is there somebody I could have a word with?'

'Aye, what is it?' Nick put his book down regretfully.

'Is the manager about?'

'He's not, no. I've worked here for twenty years, will I do?'

'It's just that I need some information about your guests.'

'I knew the chap before you – PC Tindall – he was a good bloke.'

'He's retired, I expect.'

'I should retire. I've got my allergy back. Look. . . '

The policeman looked wonderingly at Nick's unmarked hands. 'On duty last night, were you?'

'Ask me the last night I wasn't on duty.'

'Does that mean yes?' the policeman said with gathering impatience.

'No need to be short.'

'We found a Cortina wrapped around a lamp post.'

'No. I don't drive.'

'Now look, Grandad, give us a break.' He adopted a pleading tone.

'Yeah, the difference see. PC Tindall, he knew everybody, knew everything. Knew my first name, always remembered it.'

'Yeah, I know, and he had a bicycle and whistled. Is the manager in?'

'No.'

'No. You've been very helpful.' He hurried out, unable to take any more.

'I don't think I'm the thieving type,' repeated Frank as he looked at himself in the mirror. 'Do you?'

Ken shrugged. 'Well. . . ' Then he saw that Frank was obviously very depressed indeed so he thawed a bit. 'How's the leg?'

'Terrible. I'm feeling very low to be honest, Ken. I feel like I've been in a dish-washer.'

'You still can't remember what happened last night?'

'I can't. I don't know; maybe I'll wake up tomorrow and it will all come flooding back to me.'

'The first thing, I think, is to find you somewhere to stay.'

'I'm all right here. And you're next door.'

'Yeah, but I think Harry – Mr Crawford – is a bit nervous of you staying too long.'

'Wants me out, does he?' Frank was mournful.

'I think so.'

'It's a sadness all this, Ken. I have to tell you, it's a purgatory.'

'I'll have another word with him.'

'I'm a man in a mess.'

'Chin up, matey.' Ken was resolutely cheerful.

'Ken, I want to give you some of this.' He sat back in the bed and began to fiddle around under the pillow.

'Let's find out if it's yours first, eh?'

'You're a good man, Ken.'

'But if I did help you, I'm not cheap.'

'Good men never are.'

'Ken, you around?' shouted Harry from outside the door.

'Harry?'

'Where are you?'

'Coming. See you later.'

Directly he had gone Frank sank back in the bed and pulled the covers over his head.

Standing in the corridor, Harry was very insistent. 'Have you told matey he's out on his bum in the morning?'

'You mean my client?' asked Ken defensively.

Harry slowly took the description in. 'A bit of sense at last, good. I still want him out though. Remembered anything, has he?'

'No.'

'Mind you, I checked the paper – no robberies as far as I could see.'

Frank had poked his head out of the sheets to listen to their conversation. It was easy enough through the thin walls of the Grand. But after a while Frank found the conversation disappointing. He lifted the sheets and went back under again.

'Anyway,' said Harry. 'Come on and get your coat. We're going to see Fowler.'

'Let's leave it, Harry. If I see him, I'll have to hit him.'

'Just let me do the talking. We'll be fine.' He steered Ken before him, expecting resistance. Surprisingly there wasn't any. Harry drove Ken down to Fowler's yard in his beaten-up mini-van and *en route* they discussed Ken's work as a private eye.

'You see – you know you're finding it interesting.'

'Am I?'

'Fascinating. You're a trouble shooter. Different case each time.'

'Yeah.'

'So why don't you sell up?'

'What the hell for?'

'Go full-time.'

'As a private eye? No thanks. I don't like mucky cases.'

'Mucky?' Harry sounded censorious.

'Speak as you find. I'm not exactly rescuing a damsel in distress.'

'What about Mrs B?'

'That spade-wielding banshee. She's no damsel.'

'It'll come.'

'Yeah – so will the crummy divorce cases, surveillance – all that crap.'

'It's better than that boggy field.'

'You won't say that when it's got a house on it and

a thriving market garden. You'll eat your words – and my turnips.'

'Never liked turnips.'

'So you can stuff Box Thirteen – I'll only use it as a last resort.'

'Thanks.' Harry seemed quite subdued and Ken became marginally repentant.

'I know you mean well, Harry.'

'The road to hell is paved with good intentions.'

'And you're leaving me there.'

'Now look—'

'Only joking. But seriously, I am grateful.' He grinned. 'Like for the gasometer climb, like our friend without a mind—'

'A memory.'

'So he says.'

'Anyway,' said Harry, now anxious to change the subject, 'let me handle Fowler. None of your violence.'

'He attracts violence.'

'Sure – but let's try another way.'

'Is there one?'

'Yeah – my way.' Harry slowed the car down. 'And we're going my way. Right?'

'Right,' said Ken softly. 'You're a good bloke, Harry. You look after your mate, don't you?'

'Like a mother hen,' he agreed.

Ken did not take long to go on the boil. Initially the interview between Harry, Ken and Fowler had started on a somewhat apathetic note.

'You again?' asked Fowler, looking up from his desk.

'Yes,' replied Ken. 'Me again.'

'And you've brought a friend. Well, what can I do for you?'

Ignoring Fowler's deliberately offensive tone, Ken

said mildly, 'You were going to make an offer for those building materials—'

'Ah,' said Fowler, 'I was.' But when he told Ken what the offer was all hell broke loose. Ken threw himself at Fowler's throat and Harry also entered the mêlée, trying to haul Ken off.

'Ken!' yelled Harry as Fowler went blue in the face.

'I'll bloody murder you,' Ken assured him while Fowler could only gasp,

'Get him off me before I call the. . . ' His voice ended in a strangled gulp.

'Calm down, for Christ's sake calm down, Ken,' bellowed Harry.

Eventually Harry was able to disentangle Ken from Fowler's throat. He sat down heavily, tried to straighten his tie and return to normal breathing.

'Harry . . .' panted Ken.

'I'm not a blooming charity,' protested Fowler. 'I make my living by buying and selling. Now I've made you a good offer for some second-hand materials.'

'They're new! You sold them to me. They're untouched.' He tried to rise to his feet again but Harry pushed him back.

'Exactly so. They're second-hand.'

'I've not touched that stuff,' said Ken furiously.

'I'm sorry – that's my best offer and it's a good one.'

'Maybe we've misjudged Mr Fowler.'

'We have?' said Ken, looking at Harry unhappily.

'Well, I'm glad someone can see sense. I want to be fair; it's an unfortunate situation and I want to stress I am a great admirer of the fire service.'

'Smashing. In fact, to sum up this little meeting I'd say frankly, Ken, if Mr Fowler were on fire I wouldn't even spit on him.'

'You what?' Fowler was finding difficulty in keeping pace with events.

'This man was a hero, matey. He's actually done something useful with his life,' said Harry.

'Now just a minute. . . '

'Fair? You don't know what the word means. You've stitched Ken up good and proper.' He rose to his feet and this time it was Ken's turn to try and restrain him. He was too late. Harry grabbed Fowler by the throat and bellowed,

'Well, let me tell you—'

'Harry! Leave him.'

'Get off! Get off!' Fowler was desperate now, sure that he was being confronted by raving psychotics.

Still gripping his throat, Harry summarised the situation as he saw it.

'You come up with a fabulous deal – a fabulous deal – or else every place you go in this city someone will ask you why you ripped off a hero: a man with fire in his lungs. So get your calculator back out and put your finger on the big numbers and press. And then Ken will think about spending that figure on a new mobile home, and I want to stress I am not talking about a Portaloo.'

'This is ridiculous! It's blackmail.'

'No, no,' said Harry, releasing him. 'It's a fact, friend.'

Fowler returned to his calculator, his hand trembling slightly.

'Good man,' said Harry, winking at Ken who nodded. Between them, they seemed to have made some kind of impact.

Ken walked into the dining-room of the Grand Hotel, looking dapper in his jacket, collar and tie. Ethel was folding napkins and Harry was parading about, flushed and wearing oven gloves.

'Ooh! Ken's done up like a dog's dinner,' pronounced Ethel.

'Very smart,' added Harry.

'You too. Put 'em up Rocky – two rounds.' Ken raised his fists in a boxing pose. Harry did likewise with his hands still in the oven gloves. They sparred.

'Rubbish. No reach,' said Ken.

'Don't tell Fowler.'

'You were brilliant.'

'I was, wasn't I?'

'Did I say thank you?'

'About fifty times. Hey, you're chipper.'

'I am. I really can celebrate tonight.'

'I should come with you.'

'Yeah,' Ken struggled to sound enthusiastic.

'But I won't!' he teased.

They sparred again and Doreen suddenly appeared, looking terrific.

'You two!' she said, shaking her head. 'Like a couple of kids.'

'Oh, hi . . .'

'Don't let me stop you.'

'No, we were just . . .' His voice tailed away as he took in how well she was turned out. 'You look very . . . er . . .'

'Smashing – I think is the word,' said Harry.

'Thank you. You're not so bad yourself.'

'Now have a nice time,' said Harry.

'We will.'

'I've had to tell Ken that I can't join you,' said Harry, resuming his winding-up.

'Oh dear,' said Doreen.

'See, it's me and Ethel and the lasagne.' He turned to Ethel. 'Eh, love?'

'That's right,' said Ethel.

'What a fate,' sighed Harry.

There was a happy, carefree atmosphere in the car as Doreen drove Ken to the restaurant.

'So you'll be back living like a gypsy?' she asked him.

'Oh no. It isn't a caravan as such. It's a big old site office. It's very big, very solid. And I owe it all to Harry.'

'He was dying to help you out with Fowler.'

'He was the muscle, I was the brains. I just sat back.'

'You should have let *me* go with you.'

'That's what Harry said.'

'Oh yes – I specialise in character assassination, me.'

'Well you look very nice on it.'

'Drop off.'

'Listen, when a boy's buying his own dinner he can say what he likes.'

'Fair enough.' Something suddenly caught her attention. 'Now isn't that amazing!'

'What?'

'After I dropped you off last night I passed here and there was a car half-way up that lamp post. And now it's gone.'

'Fire brigade cut 'em up, cut 'em out and cart 'em away.'

'You and your fire brigade. By the way Nick says the police have been round to the hotel, making routine enquiries as they say.'

'Have they?' muttered Ken thoughtfully.

'So you think our unwanted guest in number five and the smashed Cortina might be connected?'

They were sitting in a small French restaurant whose tables were crowded close together.

'It's possible,' said Ken.

'And do you believe him?' she said as the waiter poured white wine into her glass.

'That he's lost his memory? I think I do actually.' But he looked as if he was half joking. 'But then I'm gullible. And it's hard not to like him, though he is beginning to pong a bit.'

Doreen raised her glass. 'To your new home.'

'Thanks,' said Ken. He looked around him. 'It's posh here, isn't it?'

'It's quite posh. I had too many years in the third division. No more.'

'There are a lot of nice people in the third division.' He glanced down at the arsenal of cutlery at his place setting. 'A dinner service each, is it?'

'Where have you been, Ken Boon?' said Doreen, laughing affectionately.

'The third division, mostly.'

'Well, now you're going to be a gentleman farmer, well, gardener.'

'That's right.'

'Did you always want to do that?'

'Run a market garden? No, I wanted to be a cowboy but there was no call for it down our road.'

'You'd have made a good cowboy.'

'Do you think so?'

'Is that what the fire service was all about?'

'In a way. You got to wear a big hat and do stupid things. Anyway, I know about me. What about you?'

'Nothing to tell. I'm an open book.'

'What sort of book?'

'Hardback.' She grinned at him.

'Good story?'

'A long one.'

'Okay. Chapter one: Doreen Evans was born in a small town near . . .'

'Here comes the food,' she said quickly.

But Ken was persistent. 'Where do you live? You know – since you broke up with your husband?'

The food arrived and Doreen said, 'None of your business.' But she wasn't being aggressive.

'Okay.' He looked down at a large plate of squid. 'Are you sure I'm going to like this?'

'I know you are.'

Ken still regarded it doubtfully. 'I'm sure I am,' he said, tucking in gingerly.

As he ate Doreen said, 'Just one or two things I'd like to get straight, Mr Boon.'

'Yeah?'

'Like about me.'

'I know what you're going to say.'

'Am I that predictable?'

'No. It's just that I've always felt the same. Once you've got a goal, you don't want any commitments.'

'I *am* predictable.'

'Look – you've had a bad time. You've got a new career in front of you. You can't lose sight of that.'

She looked awkward. 'I wasn't—'

'You were wondering if a lonely ex-fireman had intentions on you.'

'No.'

'And you were wondering how quick I'd show 'em.'

'You make me sound awful.' She was really flustered now.

Ken laughed and took her wrist. He squeezed it gently. 'I'm the Lone Ranger,' he said. 'Run a mile when anyone gets too close. You're the same. At the moment,' he added.

'I put everything into my marriage. And I lost everything.'

'You can't blame yourself for that.'

'I don't. I blame that bastard. Except I never knew he was.'

'What?'

'A bastard.'

Ken laughed. 'You want to get on your feet like I

do. You croupier; me market gardener. Right now we're both in training.'

'And we've got our extra-mural activities. Me part-time accountant; you part-time private eye.'

'Being what we don't want to be.'

'Oh, I don't know. I quite enjoy it. Besides, I wouldn't have met you if it hadn't been that way.'

'Mm.'

'What are you thinking about?'

'I'm thinking that squid might grow on me.' He took another doubtful bite. 'Might.' He chewed some more. 'Of course, however committed we are to our futures, there's no reason why—'

'Don't say it.'

'Say what?'

'Say we can be " good friends".'

'Oh, I wasn't going to say that . . . but I reckon that old cliché's what both of us need most right now.'

'You're right,' said Doreen, raising her glass. 'Here's to it.'

'What's the toast?'

'To old clichés,' she said. 'May they live for ever!'

But Ken was not the only would-be detective. There was Frank himself. Lying in bed, chewing Ethel's lasagne, he worked away with a big felt tip and a sheet of paper which had covered his supper tray. He was writing down Christian names in a desperate attempt to remember who he was. He had already gone through the As to the Es without success. Now he had graduated to the Fs and the Gs. He wrote Fergus, Frank, Gary, Gordon, Graham. Suddenly he went back to stare at the name Frank, and he very slowly circled the name. Then he said it aloud several times. Gradually he became enthusiastic, then excited, as he tried different inflections, speaking to himself in the mirror.

'Frank . . . Frank . . . Frank! . . . Francis . . . Frank. Frankie! Frank.' Slowly he lay back on the bed. 'I'm getting there,' he whispered.

Chapter Eight

Next morning Ken was standing in his field looking pleased with himself. Slowly his new caravan backed into view. It was a vast ancient tourer, a site office for Fowler's building company. Painted battleship grey, it had a few touches of light rust running down its sides. But generally it was in good condition and more than ample for Ken's needs. On the door a painted sign still read 'Site Office' in faded letters and on the shutters the words 'Fowlers Ltd' could just be seen. Ken signalled the driver to back the caravan in and then he helped to uncouple the truck.

When they had finished the driver came over with a clipboard and began to tick off the building supplies Ken had sold back to the unwilling Fowler. 'Common stocks, breeze blocks, windows – pink primed – cement . . .'

'That's fine,' said Ken triumphantly. All this was like a new lease of life to him.

'Oh by the way,' said the driver. 'Fowler threw in a load of green paint. He thought you wouldn't like to have his name all over it.'

He turned abruptly away as Ken began to laugh uproariously.

McGeary, the truculent forty-year-old car dealer who had been Ken's tormentor at the casino, arrived in typical form at the Grand.

'Hello, sweetheart. Must be my lucky day. Eleven o'clock in the morning and here I am face to face with a gorgeous woman.'

Doreen's reaction to his sexism was icy as she sat behind reception. 'Fancy,' she said.

'I wonder if you're going to make me even happier and come up with a bit of information?'

'I wonder.'

'Name's McGeary – McGeary's Used Cars. I'm looking for a friend.'

'Yes, I imagine that could be a problem,' said Doreen, drily.

He was momentarily taken aback and laughed brashly to cover his confusion. 'That's right. I like a girl with a bit of spirit.'

'Jolly good. Now did you want a room or are you just at a loose end?' Her voice was briskly dismissive.

'This friend, Irish chappie, a bit gormless, dark hair . . . lots of teeth. Mean anything to you?'

'No.'

'I just wanted a word with him.'

'Well, he's not here.'

'I couldn't have a quick look at the register?'

'No you couldn't.'

'Come on, don't be difficult.'

'It's what I'm best at. Are you good at anything?'

Nick walked over with his usual ambling gait. 'Having any trouble, Doreen?'

'No.'

'Who's this? Your grandad?' asked McGeary contemptuously.

Nick gave him a beatific smile. 'No one talks to me like that,' he said and began a geriatric advance on a surprised McGeary.

'Get out,' said Doreen, 'or I'll ring the police.'

Still Nick advanced, his fists upraised, still McGeary stood his ground. Doreen looked wildly around. Where the hell was Harry? Then McGeary, broadly smiling, decided to bide his time.

'I'll be back,' he said, winking lasciviously at her, 'And I'll get what I want. I always do.'

'Not here you won't,' she said.

'And look after your grandad,' said McGeary as he went out. 'Wouldn't want him to pop off.'

Ken must have passed McGeary on the street without recognising him, for when he poked his head round the door of the Grand a few minutes later Doreen let fly.

'Someone called about your client,' said Doreen. 'Someone nasty.'

'Yes,' said Nick. 'I had to sort him out.'

'You?' asked Ken in surprise.

'Me.'

'He was wonderful – he was a hero.' Doreen looked at Nick with a new respect. 'He stood up for me.'

'Who to?'

'This awful man called McGeary came in – very flash, about forty – a car salesman – and started chatting me up. Then he said he was looking for a friend.'

'Irish chappie,' repeated Nick. 'A bit gormless, dark hair, lots of teeth.'

'Seems to fit your client's description in number five quite well.'

'I don't know,' demurred Ken. 'I don't think he's gormless exactly. And it amuses me the way you've all decided that he's definitely my problem.'

'Does it?' asked Doreen. 'Anyway he's attracting the wrong kind of attention. We can't have people like that coming in here – gives the hotel a bad name.'

'That's right,' said Nick. 'And no one can expect me to be a bouncer. Not at my age.'

'No,' said Ken, 'not at your age.'

'Who's bouncing who?' breezed Harry as he came in from the kitchens.

Doreen told him, with expansive inventions from Nick, whilst he listened silently and gloomily. This development was bound to cause a lot of problems.

'This can't go on, Nick.' He turned to Ken. 'This can't go on,' he repeated.

'I thought that's what you'd say.'

'That guy's a liability.'

'I'm working on it.'

'Yeah.'

'You mean I'm not producing results quickly enough?' For the first time for ages there was tension between the two old friends.

'I didn't say that.'

'So you want him out. Where do you suggest? My caravan?'

'Now, that's not a bad idea.'

'Look, give me a bit of time. I have to find out who he is, and with this bloke coming in I've got a lead.'

'And we've got a pain in the arse,' said Harry. 'I'm trying to build up a hotel – not a crook's hideaway.'

'Who says he's a crook?' asked Ken belligerently.

Doreen intervened. 'Harry, give them a bit longer. He's almost cracked it.'

'Oh, super sleuth. OK, I'll give you time.' Harry grinned, friendlier now, regretting his irritation.

'Thanks,' said Ken bleakly. 'By the way—'

'Yeah?'

'Whose idea was this Box Thirteen business anyway?'

'You want to open the window a bit.' Ken looked round room five with distaste. Frank had left his mark.

'Okay.'

'Next time I'm out I'll buy you a pair of socks.'

'Ken, I've remembered some things.' He was childishly optimistic.

'Yeah?'

'I think my name is Frank and I think I support West Brom.'

'Well, that narrows the field,' said Ken, laughing cynically.

But Frank remained deadly serious. 'Yeah. It does, doesn't it?'

'How about Cortinas and used-car salesmen?' asked Ken.

'Do you think I'm a car salesman?' asked Frank indignantly, getting off the bed and going over to the mirror. 'I don't think so,' he said as he regarded himself objectively.

'No, but I think you might have something to do with a Cortina which did some heavy petting with a lamp post round the corner. And I think you've just had a visit from an unhappy car salesman.'

'Are you kidding me, Ken?'

'No.'

'Someone asking for me?'

'I think so.'

'Oh my God. This morning?'

'Yeah.'

'Oh my God!' he repeated 'What have I done? Who is he? How did he know I was here?'

'He doesn't. He described you, but he doesn't know you're here. But my guess is that you came from that crashed car and he's checking the area for you.'

Frank looked terrified. 'It sounds awful.'

'At least it's another piece in the jigsaw.'

'Not a very nice jigsaw.'

'Cheer up.'

'Have I still got to go this morning? I don't think I can. I'm ailing – in the mind and the body.' He lay back on the bed miserably.

'I think the best thing is to find out what this chap knows about you. He obviously does know you.'

'Sounds worse.'

'Listen, we don't even know if you've done anything wrong.'

'I must have done. I feel guilty. I've got a lot of money and . . .' He was interrupted by a knock at the door. Frank looked terrified. 'Don't answer,' he whispered.

The knock was repeated. After a minute's silence they heard Doreen's voice, muffled through the door. 'Ken?'

Hurriedly Ken opened the door. 'Doreen, this is Frank, we think. Frank, this is Doreen.'

'Hallo.'

'Hallo, Doreen.'

'So you're McGeary's friend?'

'Tom McGeary mean anything to you?' asked Ken vigorously, but Frank shook his head.

'It's true, is it? You've really lost your memory?'

Frank nodded mournfully.

Doreen spoke quickly and unhappily. 'Does anybody mind if I open the window?' She just couldn't bear it any longer.

'Sorry,' said Frank.

'I'll go and have a word with Mr McG.'

'You're mad, Ken.'

'Why do you say that?' said Frank, puzzled.

'Because this McG is obviously big trouble.'

'Is he?' Frank looked terrified again. 'Oh Christ!'

'Then I'll have to be very canny.' Ken grinned. 'It's not so brave really. I can just go and look at his cars, eh?'

'On your head be it,' said Doreen. 'Anyway, I'd better get back to reception. Are you comfortable?' she asked Frank sarcastically.

'I am, but I've had my marching orders from your manager.'

'I'll talk to him,' she said with sudden warmth. 'You'll be all right until we get this thing sorted out.'

'You're good to me, you lot.' There was a pause, then he added in a wheedling tone, 'Doreen—'

'Yes?'

'You couldn't sneak me up a bottle of the gold liquid?'

'I'm sorry?'

'Whisky.'

'I expect so,' she replied a little reluctantly.

'Bless you.'

'You're a lucky boy, aren't you?' said Ken. 'Now I'd better go and see who you are.'

'Be careful, Ken,' said Frank.

'Yes,' Doreen echoed. 'For God's sake be careful. Why the hell are you doing all this?' she added when they had left Frank's room and were walking downstairs together.

'I told you last night. I want something. Nothing much. A bit of land . . . a bit of a house. . . . And I'm learning it costs money. And if it means running around on a wild goose chase, fair enough.'

'Now there's something else I really can't stand,' she said. 'Geese.'

While Ken and Doreen slowly went downstairs, Frank burrowed back into his lair.

'You be careful,' repeated Doreen emphatically.

'Are you concerned about me, Doreen?' he asked her in a teasing voice.

'Not in the slightest. I just can't stand heroes.'

As Ken drove his motor bike through the streets of the inner city, he wondered about Doreen. For the first time in his life he found that he was desperate to make one stable relationship. Throughout his years in the fire service he had relied on the lads for company and girls for one-night stands. It had been the sexist pattern of his life and it had suited him. Now all that was changed. Echoes of the conversation in the restaurant returned to him and again he heard himself tell Doreen how independent they must be – to achieve their goals, to win their new careers.

What, however, had sounded so good in the restaurant, now seemed bleak and desolate. It was all very well to go their own separate ways, to remain friends, but actually Ken wanted far more than that – and he was beginning to realise it every day. Ponderosa was a wonderful piece of self-sufficiency – if it ever came off. But whatever happened, it would be an isolated little patch with a table permanently set for one. What did she really want? he wondered. Was she as undecided as he was? Well, thought Ken, one thing's certain. I don't exactly see her dropping her training as a croupier and coming to work at Ponderosa as the contemporary equivalent of a land girl.

And now he was in his day job – an amateur investigator combing the area for a second-hand car salesman who might, just might, reveal Frank's identity but was much more likely to do personal and lasting injury to himself. For some hours he toured the second-hand car sites, searching for McGeary, not even knowing if the business would be under his name. There had been no sign of anything to do with McGeary and second-hand cars in the phone book and all the car sales sites he visited boasted no knowledge of him whatsoever. Eventually he began to become dazed by the rows of shiny second-hand cars with their glaring price stickers and dozens of announcements extolling their virtues. Stan's Autos, Honest John's, Bargain Cars, Mick's Motors – the sites seemed endless and negative. Then, round about lunch-time, an exhausted Ken struck oil on the ramshackle premises of Autorama.

'Can I help you, sir?' The salesman was as down at heel as his cars, some of which were all too obviously unroadworthy. There were others in a tumbledown shed beside the forecourt. They looked worse.

'I'm looking for a chap called McGeary.'

'Not here, sir.'

'He's a car salesman – with his own business.'

'You could ask my manager.' He turned round to a semi-ruined Portacabin and bellowed 'Mum!'

There was no response and although he bellowed again nothing happened.

'You'd better come over. She's probably having a kip,' said the young man apologetically.

Ken followed him wearily and they eventually arrived in the dark shadows of the broken building. 'She's in there,' he said, spotting a possible punter and legging it swiftly towards him.

It was dark inside the hut, so dark that he could hardly make out the shape inside that seemed rooted to the armchair. All he could see was the glow of a cigarette.

'What d'you want?'

The voice was rasping, grating. As his eyes got used to the dark, Ken could make out the ancient features of 'Mum'. Clad in a rag-bag assortment of cardigans, she had a packet of twenty Benson and Hedges in front of her and a half-consumed bottle of stout.

'Excuse me,' said Ken. 'I'm looking for a Mr McGeary, and your son said you might help.'

'Who does he think I am? A telephone directory?'

'Being in the car trade – ' Ken's voice was low with respect.

''E's in the trade, is 'e, McGeary?'

'Yeah – but I don't know if he operates under his own name.'

She all but smiled. 'And if I do know him. What then?'

'You might tell me.'

'And I might not.'

Ken sighed.

'Ain't I seen you before?' the old crone said suddenly. 'Ain't you a smokie?'

'Well – yes—'

'John Goodwin – you know him? My elder son.'

'John – of course I do. Used to be in White Watch with him.'

'Sit down.' Her voice, still rasping, was friendly. Ken sat down on a springless sofa. 'You look all in.'

'I am.'

'Must 'ave seen you at a social.'

'Yeah.'

'Good socials, those fire brigade ones. Plenty of booze.' She cackled. 'Why you lookin' for McGeary?'

'It's a long story.'

'Tell me.'

Ken told her, leaving out the bit about the money.

'I'll tell you this,' she said. 'McGeary's trouble. But I'll help you. I can't tell you where he is, but I can send you to someone who does. 'Course she may not tell you.'

'Who is she?'

''Is Mum.'

'Another mum?'

She chortled. 'Mum's outing.'

'What's that supposed to mean?'

'I'm coming with you.'

'I've only got a motor bike,' said Ken.

'What type?'

'BSA A65. 650cc.'

'What do you call it?'

'Lightning.'

'Good name. I used to have one of them back in the sixties. Always on it. My old man used to drive a Morris Traveller.' She cackled again. 'Got a pillion?'

'Yeah.'

'Come on then.' She heaved up her vast bulk, drained the stout and grabbed the fags. 'Let's go and find Maureen. What's your name, love?'

'Ken.'

'Mine's Rose. Come on.'

'Doesn't this move?'

They were chugging through the traffic at about forty miles an hour with Rose sitting relaxed on the pillion, helping to balance the bike with her vast bulk. From somewhere she had dragged out an ancient crash helmet and it rested uneasily on her large head. She had a fag in, which was dangerously close to Ken's ear.

'There's a speed limit.'

She grunted and was quiet for a mile or so.

'Draw over,' she said suddenly.

'Eh?'

'I said, draw over.'

Obediently Ken drove on to the pavement. There was less traffic now and the road was wider.

'We're gonna swop.'

'What?'

'Come on. Get off. Or you won't get anywhere near Maureen.'

'All right.' He scrambled off and swopped with her. As she mounted the saddle, Rose lit yet another cigarette.

'Okay?'

'Yes,' said Ken, closing his eyes.

Back at the Grand, Doreen and Harry were deep in conversation.

'I just don't want to come in full time, love. I really don't.'

Harry groaned. 'It's the reception area. You bring up the tone. Nick isn't exactly charismatic.'

'No,' she had to agree. 'Can't you afford another part-time receptionist?'

He shrugged. 'Sure, but it's the personality.'

'You're very flattering.'

'I'm very desperate.'

'I'm determined to be a croupier.'

'So if I ran a casino here how would that be?' He sounded excited. 'Or wouldn't it be classy enough?'

She smiled at him. 'It's not that, love. You wouldn't get a licence.'

'Me personally?'

'No, the Grand. There can only be one casino in a certain radius. And I'm there.'

'Oh well . . . I s'pose I'll lose you altogether soon.'

Doreen sighed. 'Not at the rate I'm going. I won't be leaving for years yet. I keep making mistakes.'

'You'll learn.'

'I hope so.'

'And then I'll be stuck with Box Thirteen – Ken and Nick.'

'That's a bit unfair.'

'I know that.'

'After all, Box Thirteen was your idea.'

'So everyone keeps reminding me. Now I've got a freak upstairs that I can't get rid of in a room I can't let which will need fumigating and de-lousing anyway.'

'I believe in Ken. He's going to be all right.'

'As a market gardener?'

'As a self-employed bloke. He's got guts and initiative. Great loss to the brigade.'

'So am I,' said Harry.

Meanwhile, Rose thundered on at 70 mph with Ken's voice a constant protest in her left ear. But she paid him no heed as they tore off a corner at a 45 degree angle and almost ended up under a bus.

'This brings back the old days,' she shrieked, alarmingly turning her head round towards him.

'Watch out!'

Skirting a truck, she came to an abrupt halt outside an amusement arcade – so abrupt that Ken almost parted company with his pillion. When the dust had settled she said:

'This is Maureen's place.'

Nick and Ethel were sitting talking in the kitchen, debating the future of the Grand.

'I don't like the changes he's making,' grumbled Nick. 'This hotel had class in them old days. Now he's bringing in plastic chairs and we got a bloke from the funny farm in room five. Crooks coming and going—'

'I've worked in hotels all my life,' chimed Ethel, 'and never seen the like. I worked in London during the war and met my Tom. He was assistant chef at the Savoy, he was.'

'Died young, didn't he?' said Nick morbidly. He loved talking about death and he had a fellow enthusiast in Ethel.

'Died young, died suffering. You've never seen the like at the end. He weighed three stone and his skin was parchment. You could put your finger through it.'

Nick nodded. 'My old Dad went that way.'

'Then we had the restaurant. That was a classy place. Jack o' Lantern in Five Trees. My Tom did those steaks so tender . . . and I raised my three.'

'Never been blessed,' said Nick. He paused. 'Then I never been married. Like poor old Ken.'

'He's a one.'

'Think he's setting his cap at Doreen?'

'He tries – he tries—'

'Am I breaking anything up?' asked Harry as he came in for a cup of tea.

'No,' said Nick, pouring him out a cup. 'Just chatting over old times.'

Pin ball and fruit-machines clattered, electronic games bleeped. The place was full of floating lights and pools of darkness and young kids bunking off school. Maureen was younger than Rose, a big square woman with a flourishing moustache. She was squeezed into a tiny plywood box which bore the legend CHANGE GIVEN HERE. Her eyes looked caged and they moved from Ken's to Maureen's face as if watching a tennis match. They were small, suspicious, calculating.

'Well?'

'He wants your boy.'

There was fear – a protective fear – in her eyes now. 'You the filth?'

'No,' said Ken. 'I'm – acting on behalf of a friend of his.'

'You're a dick.'

'Eh?'

'Private detective.'

'Leave it out,' said Rose. 'You gonna help him or not?'

'I still don't know what you want him for.'

'There's a bloke he wants to get in touch with.'

'Yeah?'

'Urgent like.'

'I see. Well, seeing as how you're not the filth or a dick I'll tell you.'

She wrote down an address on a grubby piece of paper and shoved it to him under the grille. 'Give him my love.'

'Sure – and – ' Ken hesitated. 'Would you do me another favour?'

'What?' She looked suspicious again as he produced a fiver and shoved it through to her.

'Take this.'

'What for?'

'Have a good reunion with Rose. Couple of gins.'

'But I wanted to come on your bike.'

'I know, love, but I can't take it again. I haven't the nerve. Thanks for everything.' Ken turned and fled.

Half an hour later Ken arrived on the edge of a sprawling housing estate. Checking the address, he drove through the estate until he found a nest of rather tatty shops and, on the corner, a secondhand car lot. It was small and as tatty as its surroundings. Ken's confidence received a further boost – McGeary's manner may have been brash, but his background was of mean streets. He really couldn't be that successful nor, perhaps, that powerful. Of course, he could still be tough and nasty.

Ken dismounted, leaving the bike parked by the side of the battered awning that displayed the more up-market of McGeary's cars. Then, as he walked towards the office, he stopped dead in his tracks. He could hear the far from dulcet tones of McGeary talking on the telephone, slightly distorted by a gusty wind which rattled litter around the pavements.

'And you described the little dough bag . . .' His voice faded. 'Everywhere. Brilliant . . .' His voice faded again. 'What d'you mean, must have left town? I'd be surprised if he could even bloody crawl. Have you seen the car? He had a bloody lamp post in the back seat . . .'

As Ken walked over to the lot he saw the wretched Cortina standing on the forecourt. He quickened his pace and McGeary's voice became clearer.

'That's sweet. So when I want intelligence I'll know where to go . . . Yeah, sure . . .' He mimicked someone's voice,' "Sorry, boss." Listen, get off your arse and find the little bugger, or you'll . . . Wait a minute – ' He saw Ken walking towards him. 'Here's a customer. Call me when you've got something.' He hung up and breezed out of the shack-like office. 'Good afternoon, sir, and what can I do for you?' He obviously hadn't recognised him from their brief encounter in the casino.

'I was looking for a car, actually.'

'You couldn't have come to a better place. This is a car showroom.' He laughed loudly at his own feeble joke.

'I hear that Cortinas are really good value.'

'Our speciality, sir.'

Ken glanced at the stove-in car. 'Only one owner?'

'Not our best advertisement I must admit.' He paused. 'How about a stroll around the estate then, sir. And tell me, why should a motor-cycling man want to give up all that excitement for the thinking person's motor?'

'You know how it is. We all have to settle down eventually.'

They paced up and down between the serried ranks of used cars, while Ken plotted his next move.

'How about this, sir? It's a beauty. Belonged to the wife. Broke her heart when I took it.' McGeary pointed to a superficially gleaming saloon.

'Sunday car, was it?'

'Got her a new Jag in exchange, and she still wanted to hang on to this one.'

Ken shrugged and they walked on in uneasy silence. Finally they returned for the second time to the crashed Cortina.

'Are you sure it's a car you're after?' McGeary was suddenly suspicious.

'How do you mean?' asked Ken innocently.

'Well, I've taken you round the place twice and nothing seems to take your fancy.'

'Er—'

'Sure you shouldn't still be looking for a bike?' he said, glancing towards Ken's bike. He still seemed to be in a good mood – relatively speaking. 'That's a nice bit of work and no mistake. Go all right?'

'Not brilliant,' said Ken. 'Needs a lot of lousy attention.'

'But when it is going?'

'It goes a treat.'

'So – ' McGeary paused. 'So – ' He cleared his throat. 'This car—'

Ken was now at a loss. He was finding it impossible to bring McGeary on to the subject of Frank with any kind of subtlety – if at all. 'Have you got a Fiesta?'

'We passed about six of 'em. Anyway, as it happens, I've got a super little car over here. Very low mileage—'

They were passing the wrecked car again. 'Puts you off a bit, doesn't it?'

'Eh?'

'Having this on the forecourt.'

'So you said before,' commented McGeary with increasing irritation and suspicion.

'It's like a kind of bad advert.'

'Yeah.'

'I mean, you'd be a lucky man to walk away from that.'

'You would indeed.'

'You know him, do you?' said Ken, taking the plunge.

'Where've I seen you before?'

'Me?'

'You're one of Frank's mates, aren't you?'

'Could be.'

'You work with that toe rag on the rigs, don't you?'

'Not me.'

'Yes you do. You tell him from me – brother-in-law or no brother-in-law – he's for the bloody high jump.'

'Right. Well, thanks for the . . .' He began to move cautiously away, realising he had blown it, too fast too soon. Some private eye, thought Ken gloomily.

'So where is he? What's this meant to be? Peace talks? Because there's no peace, sonny.'

'I'll tell him,' said Ken hastily, still moving away but with greater speed.

'Oh no. I'll tell him – and you can take me.' He whistled loudly and two large men appeared from behind the office. Both looked extremely sinister. 'Get on down here!' McGeary shouted. 'We've got a comedian here who knows where Frank is.'

After pausing for a fraction of a second, Ken took off with the three of them in pursuit. Almost at once Ken seemed, inexplicably, to disappear amongst the rows of gleaming cars. His pursuers gathered for a hasty conference.

'Who is he, boss?'

'Some contact of Frank's, Gerry. A right trouble-maker. Come to suss us out.'

'What are we gonna do?' asked the other heavy.

'Patrick, my dear boy, we're going to give him a beating. The soundest beating he's ever had. But we've got to find him first. Get it?'

They nodded.

'Now, split up and look under the cars.'

Ken, meanwhile, had relied on his native wit. He had squeezed himself between two cars with his feet off the ground. It was a temporary and uncomfortably unreliable hiding place. To secure his hidey-hole it was necessary to close his eyes in total concentration, and he could only sense what was going on around him. How long could he stay like this? he wondered.

Gerry walked down the length of the cars, his hands dangling down by his hips, rather like a Wild West gunfighter. Every avenue spelt danger and he walked slowly, precisely, checking every gap and doorway. The other two did the same, but it was Gerry's good fortune to see the suspended man, trance-like in his concentration. Slowly he began to creep up on him, and Ken appeared not to hear anything of his lumbering footfalls.

Ken's concentration was so great that his natural antennae for quick reactions let him down completely. He was in a void, oblivious to everyone. That made it very easy for Gerry to pad over to him and tap him on the shoulder. With a violent start, Ken opened one eye and fell to the ground.

'You stupid git!'

Gerry stood over Ken, his fist upraised. 'What you doing?'

'Practising levitation,' said Ken, 'and cheating with it.'

'Now you're bloody for it,' remarked Gerry, getting ready to put the boot in.

'Hang about.'

'Eh?'

'How about this for upward levitation?' With considerable effort, Ken jumped up from his crouching position and swung his crash helmet hard, cracking Gerry across the face. Gerry went down, poleaxed, with a muttered cry and Ken hurriedly but discreetly began to move away.

'You hear that?' Pat bent an ear to the wind and McGeary paused impatiently.

'What?'

'I thought I heard something. A cry.'

'I didn't hear nuthin', boss.'

'You wouldn't.'
'Where's Gerry?'
'Searching.'
'I don't see his head.'
'Perhaps he's looking at the ground.'
'Oh Gawd – come on.'

Wheezing slightly, Ken raced down the lines of cars while his pursuers circled the lot warily. Gently he opened the door of the huge estate car and tucked himself down under the steering column. Slowly he pulled the door to but didn't latch it. Then he settled down gingerly, his body arched in tension, watching through the rear-view mirror McGeary and his heavy walking towards the car. Then they began to walk away.

Smiling to himself, Ken pushed against the door, only to find that something had jammed. In panic he pushed again and accidentally switched on the hazard warning flashers.

'There's the bastard!' yelled McGeary, and they began to pound towards him. Ken just managed to dodge their by now infuriated attentions and ran off, wheezing more heavily, to the edge of the car park. But his lack of lung power slowed him down considerably. Gradually McGeary and Pat gained ground. Several times he gained a few yards – but no more than that. Meanwhile his breath was coming in short sharp stabs and Ken felt he would collapse at any moment.

McGeary and Pat were inches from him now and Ken knew that he was finished. Then, as he ground to a halt, Ken saw he was facing a half-washed car. On the bonnet was a sponge, a bucket of soapy water and a chamois leather.

So this was to be his last stand, thought Ken, and Custer, standing cool-eyed before his enemy, flashed through his mind. With admirable dexterity he grabbed a large card from the car windscreen marked GREAT OFFER. He flicked it at Pat. For a few seconds the card spiralled and they all watched its progress with fascination. Then it caught Pat under the nose, causing considerable pain and total collapse. His hands to his nose, Pat wailed, whilst McGeary yelled, 'Get on with it, you big pouf!'

To the accompaniment of Pat's agony Ken then picked up the bucket and flung the contents, soapsuds and all, over them both. It was such a sudden move that it took them completely by surprise.

'Gawd!' McGeary slipped and fell struggling to the asphalt whilst Pat, still clutching his nose, found the soapsuds exacerbated the pain. 'Get him!' shrieked McGeary. 'Just get him.' But Pat stayed, dabbing away at his face miserably.

'You're both wet behind the ears,' provoked Ken, as he took in the scene of soapy devastation with considerable satisfaction.

'I'll get you for this!' yelled McGeary as he struggled clumsily to his feet, coughing and spluttering and lunging ineffectually at Ken, who backed off, stumbling away in the direction of his bike. This time his breathing was easier, less pumping, but he was still wheezing badly. As he ran, Ken realised how stupid he had been. If only he hadn't paused to watch his assailants' plight he could have been on his bike. Now, unfortunately, they had gained a second wind, spurred on by their manic rage at what he had done to them.

Kicking over a pile of rusty oil cans, he managed to delay them fractionally. Diving out of the entrance Ken jumped on his bike, tried to kick-start it, and failed. There was nothing except a faint, cheerless, unbearably frustrating whirring sound.

He kick-started again – but with no luck and looking up he saw his pursuers were gaining, their vision improving, their tempers boiling.

'Come on, Lightning! This is no time to be temperamental,' he hissed at his bike as he tried again. Still nothing. Meanwhile McGeary and Pat were within feet of him, murder in their eyes. 'Please.' He stroked White Lightning's petrol tank. 'Please.' Still nothing. His hopes fading, he tried again – and the engine miraculously fired, roaring away from the grasping fingers of McGeary.

'I'll have you,' he bayed as Ken put vital distance between him and his pursuers. 'I'll have you –' McGeary's voice floated after him. 'Make no mistake about it.'

'On my mother's life,' screamed Pat, waving a cumbersome fist. 'You'll die for what you've done today.'

'Live now, pay later,' yelled Ken, waving derisively at the receding couple.

Just then Gerry hobbled miserably up.

McGeary surveyed his lieutenants cynically, one with streaming red eyes, and the other with a bruised and bloodied face. 'Pathetic,' he said. 'Absolutely pathetic,' he added unsympathetically. 'I don't know why I keep you two.' McGeary watched the rapidly receding figure of Ken, two fingers still clearly upraised. 'I know that geezer from somewhere. And it'll come back to me. I'm sure it will. Meanwhile, follow him. See where he goes and report back to me.'

Chapter Nine

There was not exactly a bustle of activity when Ken returned to the Grand. Doreen was in her usual place behind reception and there was a general air of tatty tranquillity. Then the phone rang and Doreen answered it with alacrity. Another booking. Things were looking up. She was taking down the details when Ken arrived, looking exhausted but well pleased with himself.

'You look all in,' she hissed, one hand over the mouthpiece.

'I almost was.'

'Still in one piece?'

'Just about.'

'What have you been up to?'

'Just getting to know Frank's family.'

'Hallo, Smokie.' Harry appeared armed with an army of light bulbs. He went behind the desk and leant on the counter. 'Who done it?' he asked.

'Follow me and find out.'

Doreen raised her eyebrows as Ken and Harry hurried upstairs. 'The dynamic duo,' she said to herself, shaking her head. Then she returned to the caller. 'We do have a vacancy on the dates you requested . . .' But as she talked her thoughts were a few yards away. In room five. Was a dramatic denouement about to take place?

Harry and Ken swept in to find a dejected Frank lying on his bed. He had a pad in front of him – and on it was scrawled one name: McGeary.

'Ah,' said Ken, looking down at it reflectively. 'Now that's a little familiar.'

'He's my brother-in-law.' Frank's voice was bleak.

'Is he now?'

'I've been looking at the name for hours.' He pointed to the pad. 'I couldn't work out why it made me so depressed. Then I remembered. It was my wife's name.

'And your brother-in-law has gone right off you. He doesn't like me much either.'

'Oh dear,' said Frank inadequately.

'What did you do to him?' asked Harry.

'I don't know.'

'Well, he didn't steal the money. It's his.' He turned to Frank. 'Yes,' he said, speaking slowly, 'the money's yours.'

'Is it?' He looked up at Ken blankly. 'You work on the oil rigs.'

'Do I?' He got up and went to the mirror. 'How do you know?'

'A little bird told me.'

Frank was still standing in front of the mirror, miserably staring at himself. 'Oh Gawd,' he said.

'What's the matter?'

'I thought I was something a bit more . . . I don't know . . . maybe dangerous.'

'Sorry about that.' Frank slunk away from the mirror, disappointed.

'So you can get paid now then, Ken?' prompted Harry.

'Absolutely. No question. I've been wanting to pay him.' Frank eagerly handed Ken a roll of five-pound notes. 'Here you are – plant it in the ground.'

Ken's heart warmed to his new client. 'I will. Thanks.'

'And you can go home now and patch it up with the missus,' Harry told Frank.

'I don't think so,' said Ken slowly.

'Oh?' Harry looked disappointed.

'I think there's a problem there.'

'Not another one,' said Frank.

'I think your family have plans for you – like entering a hospital ward.'

'I see,' said Frank with slow comprehension and a look of dawning horror in his eyes. 'Is that the brother-in-law?'

Ken nodded rather sadly.

'I don't want any violence in my hotel,' said Harry grimly, looking sourly at Ken. 'He's your client when all's said and done. I want him out.'

'Violence,' said Frank, overtaken with panic. 'Violence.'

'Guess where he stopped off at – and went inside?' asked Pat of McGeary in excited tones.

'London Zoo?'

'This a guessing game?'

'The Grand.'

'The Grand Hotel?'

'That's it. Walked in bold as brass.'

'Right. Find Gerry and we'll go straight over there.'

Pat went out of the car sales office and didn't return for some time. Eventually McGeary went to look for him. He found both his employees in earnest conversation around the wrecked car.

'And what may this be? A shop stewards' meeting?'

Pat looked up guiltily, Gerry more sullenly.

'We was thinking. If we go to the Grand, we might be in trouble.'

'You'll be in trouble if you don't.'

'I mean –' Gerry pursued his theme ponderously. 'It's not gonna help anyone if things get out of control, like.'

'They won't.'

'You gonna beat up this Ken bloke –' put in Pat.
'And the Frank bloke –' added Gerry.
'But if the filth get involved,' continued Pat, 'we could be in trouble. And I'm on probation and Gerry's on licence.'
McGeary grinned angrily at them. 'Yeah – and who is your avuncular provider?'
'Eh?'
'Who gives you the ready?'
'You do, boss,' said Pat. 'We'd like to oblige.'
'What did you have in mind, boss?' asked Gerry in a more generous spirit.
'Well,' said McGeary with greater warmth, 'I wasn't looking for a punch-up.'
'No?'
'Just a bit of sorting out.'
'And what would that involve?'
'Remonstrations. I shall press charges.'
'Yeah?' They gazed at him blankly and Gerry said, 'That could be nasty.'
'I knew there'd be violence,' said Pat.
'Only if he struggles,' insisted McGeary. 'Only in restraint or self-defence. We're going to make a citizen's arrest.'
'Yeah,' said Pat, 'that's legal, innit?'
'It most certainly is.'
'So – you'll join me. A very low key affair. Yes?'
'Yes, Boss,' they chorused.
'Right. Pat, go and pick up Sue and meet us back here. Now!'

McGeary, Pat and Gerry trooped along the road outside the Grand Hotel. They were a strange trio: McGeary with his flash suit and tie and Pat and Gerry looking dishevelled in greasy overalls. Pat had a swelling bruise under his nose and Gerry a great dark abrasion on his forehead and a bloodied mouth. Neither looked very low-profile or peaceable.

'Now,' said McGeary, wheeling on them at the hotel entrance. 'Remember this is a gentlemanly visit. We're here to extract our rights, not to start a bundle.'

His henchmen nodded uneasily as he led them in.

'Not you again,' said Doreen. 'I told you to clear off last time. Now get lost and take those two ape-men with you.'

'Wait a minute—'

'No waiting – this isn't a parking zone,' said Nick, advancing down the hallway as fast as his limp would allow him.

'Blimey,' said Pat. 'It's the old man of the sea.'

'Don't you go insulting me.'

McGeary quickly turned to Doreen. 'I'm here to see Frank Warren.'

'Who?'

'I know he's here.'

'I'm glad.'

'And I'm also anxious to speak to the man who assaulted both myself and my colleagues. He was seen to enter these premises.'

'Regular rogues gallery we've got here.'

'Madam, I'd be most grateful if you'd co-operate with me.'

'I'm afraid I can't. Why don't you phone the police if you're so worried?'

'That would hardly enhance the reputation of your hotel.'

'Better them than your two ape-men,' snapped Doreen. Pat and Gerry's eyes hardened with anger.

'What you been in?' asked Nick with a geriatric laugh. 'The boxing ring?'

'We was assaulted,' said Pat.

'Done,' said Gerry. 'And we're gonna kill him.'

'So that's it,' said Doreen.

'Now lads,' remonstrated McGeary. 'Control.'

'I'll bloody sort him,' said Gerry. 'Look what he done to me.' He pointed at the bruise on his forehead.

'You've got nothing up there to hurt,' put in Nick pleasantly.

Gerry gave a primaeval cry of rage and advanced on him. Nick calmly stood his ground.

'Lads –' said McGeary.

'I'm going to ring the police,' said Doreen emphatically.

'You're not.'

'I am.'

'You're bloody not,' roared McGeary, suddenly losing his temper. 'Get away from that phone!' But Doreen had already picked it up.

Sitting in number five with Frank and Harry, Ken suddenly heard one hell of a commotion coming from downstairs. The all-too-familiar McGeary tones could be heard loudly raised, Doreen was shouting her head off and there was inarticulate growling from the background which Ken recognised as belonging to Pat and Gerry.

'Doreen!' yelled Ken wildly as the shouting grew louder. He turned to Harry. 'Stay with him.'

'Oh my Gawd,' said Frank, burying himself once again in his sheets.

Ken raced out of the room, leaving Harry to say to Frank, 'Get off that bleeding bed!'

McGeary was looming over the reception counter, red in the face and clearly threatening, as Ken reached the top of the stairs. He was holding the phone in one hand and fending Doreen off with the other. The apes were hovering.

'I'm getting the police,' said Doreen, refusing to be intimidated.

Nick creaked in the direction of the office phone but McGeary turned and walked purposefully after him. 'You again, Grandad!'

'Don't you speak to me like that!'

'Get your paws off that phone.' Nick had shakily picked up the receiver but McGeary grabbed it, tearing it out of his hand.

'Now look—'

'Shut up, Grandad. Speak when you're spoken to.' He slammed the receiver down and when Nick made another move towards it Pat said, 'Touch it and I'll smash you.'

Doreen had already picked up the receiver again in reception but McGeary was at her side in a flash. He grabbed her wrist and held on to it savagely.

'What are we going to do?' asked Frank, his teeth chattering in fear.

'We're going to lurk,' said Harry.

'Eh?'

'On the top landing. See how Ken handles the situation – on behalf of his client.'

'Client?'

'*You*!'

'Oh yeah.' Frank looked pleased, but as they crept over the landing his fear returned.

While Frank and Harry lurked, Ken reached the bottom of the stairs. Taken by surprise, McGeary released Doreen's wrist.

'Leave her alone,' snapped Ken.

McGeary stared at him with a kind of satisfied hatred. 'So it *is* you.'

'Yeah, me.'

'Then you're for it, matey!'

'Now just calm down.'

'I want Frank – then I want you.'

'You're not going anywhere.'

Pat and Gerry looked on with interest. Showing an unusual flash of initiative they had posted themselves menacingly by the telephones.

'Get out my way.'

'I'm sorry,' said Ken. 'I'm staying in the way.'

'I want to make a citizen's arrest.'

'What?' Ken looked at him in amazement. 'A what arrest?'

'You heard. You assaulted my staff and damaged my property.'

'In self-defence.'

'That's not how we see it.'

Ken shrugged as McGeary advanced. 'Stay where you are.'

'Get out of the way.'

Suddenly Ken grabbed the fire extinguisher and pointed it as McGeary. 'I know how to use one of these.'

McGeary stepped back, returning to his semi-placating style. 'This is a family matter. I don't know what the lying little basket's told you, but he knocked hell out of my sister. No one touches her and gets away with it.'

As if on cue, an attractive young woman abruptly appeared in the foyer. Her appearance was somewhat marred by a couple of black eyes and a fat lip.

'This is Sue,' said McGeary by way of introduction. 'And she's been roughed up – done over.'

That seemed clear enough, thought Ken, as he still held them at bay with his fire extinguisher.

'Get her back in the car, Gerry,' said McGeary.

'Don't hurt him, Tom. It's my fault,' said Sue obliquely but dramatically, though to little effect.

'Frank? He's a little runt and I'm going to pulverise him,' said McGeary. 'That's a promise – if we can get rid of the fire brigade here.'

'Did Frank do that?' asked Ken, eyeing Sue's injuries. It seemed hard to believe. Surely he wasn't the type. But you never knew. Even the escapist Frank was probably capable of being roused to great passion.

'He did, and there was no need either.' McGeary sounded censorious. 'I'd already dealt with the problem. I'd run that other bastard out of town.'

'Other bastard?' asked Ken. 'So this is where P. Brandon comes in, is it?'

The effect of Ken's remark on Sue was quite startling and she turned on McGeary with sudden fury. 'How does he know about Pete? Tom – have you been telling everybody? You promised – I'm going to—'

'Shut up!' said McGeary. 'Please shut up!'

On the landing, Harry and Frank were crouched down by the banisters, listening avidly.

'Is this true?' hissed Harry, turning threateningly on Frank. 'Did you beat that young woman up?'

But Frank was not listening. His eyes were glazed and his mouth was opening and shutting wordlessly. 'It's coming back,' he said.

'Eh?'

'My past. It's all coming back.'

'*All* coming back?'

'Brandon!' Frank stood up and began to tiptoe away.

'Where are you going?' Harry followed him.

'Thinks he can move before I catch up with him!'

'What?'

'Where's the back way?'

'Hang about.'

'Harry, give us your car keys.' Frank turned on him desperately.

'What?'

'Give me your car keys!' said Frank insistently.

'Not likely.'

'Come up here.' Frank beckoned Harry up the corridor, away from the mêlée downstairs. 'Don't you see my memory's back. I'm Frank Warren, and I want to sort out an enemy. I have to do it – now.'

'Listen,' hissed Harry. 'First you move into my hotel and refuse to leave. Then you suddenly want to sign out immediately – with my car. You crazy?'

'I need transport. I'll return it.'

'No.'

'I need it fast.'

'No.'

'Let me have it.'

'No.'

'I'll pay the bill. Twice over if you like.'

'Nothing will convince me you should take my car. Not after what you did to the last one you drove.'

'I was upset.'

'I'm sorry,' said Harry, without much conviction.

'P'raps this might convince you,' said Frank unexpectedly.

Harry felt something sharp against his throat.

'What the hell?'

'It's a knife, Harry. With a very sharp blade.'

'You *are* barmy. I knew you were dangerous.'

'And don't call out or I'll stick you. I'm a dangerous man – a *very* dangerous man.'

'Nutter.'

'Put your hands above your head. Quickly.'

Slowly Harry did as he was told and the knife moved against his throat.

'What do you want me to do?'

'Move – you move up the corridor and back into room five. Right?'

'That stinking hole?'

'Come *on*!'

They advanced up the corridor, Harry with his hands above his head and Frank following him closely, holding the knife against Harry's throat. At room five they paused.

'Get in.'

Harry shambled forwards.

'Go on! Open the door and get in.'

He did so and they edged inside.

'Right,' said Frank. 'Give me your car keys.'

Reluctantly, Harry dragged his keys out of the back pocket of his trousers and Frank seized them.

'I'm sorry, Harry,' said Frank. 'I'm a man betrayed.' Still brandishing the knife, he backed towards the door, whipped out the key and was through it before Harry could get off the bed, locking the door behind him.

Downstairs the confrontation continued.

'You – get out of the way. He's got a lot to answer for. I can hear him up there,' said McGeary.

'I'm not moving.'

In answer McGeary made a dive for Doreen who quietly dodged out of the way.

'Leave her.'

Ken broke the deadlock as he raced downstairs. He threw the fire extinguisher at Pat and Gerry as they came for him, before making for McGeary. But before he could throw himself at him the sound of Harry's muffled yelling came from upstairs.

'Frank!' shouted Sue. 'Something's happened to my Frank!' She rushed for the stairs and a second frozen tableau formed. The garbled cries continued as Sue rushed on, shouting Frank's name. Then, with different degrees of speed, they followed.

Ken passed Sue on the stairs and was the first to the door of room five. It was locked. Sue followed him, still calling out Frank's name in desperation. Where was Frank? wondered Ken. Back in his room? And if so, why was Harry in there too – yelling.

'Open this bleeding door,' Harry shouted.

'Frank, Frank, are you all right?' screamed Sue, drowning Harry's voice.

'Stand back, Harry,' said Ken, hoping he would be heard above all the noise. He was just about to shoulder the door when all the others arrived on the scene.

Harry raised his voice with an even greater urgency. 'For God's sake don't damage the door. There's a spare key in number twelve. It'll fit the lock for this—'

'All *right*.'

'I've got a living to earn,' moaned Harry. 'I can't have doors broken down. How would you like it if I broke down the door of your caravan? I mean it's not a—'

Ken was already halfway up the corridor. But despite his speed it was too late, for McGeary had arrived with his two lieutenants.

'Get him out of there!' he commanded.

Sue pleaded, 'Don't hurt him, Tom . . . please . . .'

McGeary ignored her. 'Go on – break down the door,' he yelled at Pat and Gerry.

Pat and Gerry backed off down the corridor and began to lumber towards the door.

'Hold it,' shouted Ken, wrenching the key out of the lock of number twelve, and beginning to puff down the corridor.

Harry's muffled voice could be heard beseeching, 'Don't break the door. It's my . . .' The door shattered, knocking Harry back on to the bed. '. . . living.' Harry's voice tailed away as Sue pushed her way through. She presented quite a sight with her pulverised features. 'Who the hell are you?' he asked.

She ignored him. 'Frank. Where's Frank?'

'Yeah. Where is he?' said McGeary, going up to Harry menacingly, Ken hurrying along behind him.

'He held a knife against my throat, took my car keys and went out the back. He's going after Brandon.'

Instantly Ken reacted and before anyone made a move he was out of the room and belting down the stairs.

McGeary turned on his sister angrily. 'Come on. You take us there – and move it.'

They all stumbled down the stairs after her, leaving Harry glumly regarding his shattered door.

Doreen appeared in the doorway. 'Blimey,' she said. 'Ken's detective work *is* expensive.'

When Ken jumped on to Lightning, he was hoping and praying that it would start. It didn't. Looking back at the entrance to the Grand Hotel, Ken kicked again and, as usual, there wasn't a spark of life. He glanced back again, hearing shouting and the pounding of feet. Lightning started, by some miracle, just as McGeary appeared, fulminating, at the doorway.

As he sped off, McGeary shouted, 'And I'm not finished with you yet.'

'You haven't started,' Ken replied with a grin, watching the Keystone Cops entourage of McGeary, Sue, Pat and Gerry run for a beaten-up Cortina that was parked opposite. A thought flashed through his mind: there must be some way of delaying them – some really effective way. What the hell could it be? Then a plan occurred to him.

'There must be some way of knocking him out,' mused McGeary as Pat backed the car round in what must have been at least a seven-point turn. With a screech of brakes they finally faced the right way and began to tear after the distant figure of Ken.

'What shall we do, boss?' asked Gerry. 'Run him down?'

'A little crude,' said McGeary as Sue looked at Gerry aghast. 'You both crooks or something?'

'Something,' said Gerry, affronted.

'Pat, you've got the directions,' said McGeary. 'Can we get ahead of him? Take a short cut of some sort?'

'Sure, boss. I can get through on one of the estates.'

'What then?' said Gerry.

'We'll hide the car and get him before he goes in the house.'

'It's Frank I'm worried about,' said Sue.

'One thing at a time,' said her brother firmly.

When he saw the battered Cortina peeling off in his rear mirror Ken knew they were taking a short cut through one of the estates. All his cowboy instincts for danger were aroused. 'It's an ambush,' he muttered to himself, pleased. Their move exactly fitted in with his plan. Accelerating, he roared on, hoping against hope that he would attract the necessary attention. For a mile or so nothing happened and his hopes were dashed. Then he heard the wailing of a police siren.

Doreen stood with Harry and Nick, surveying the damage.

'That private eye will pay for this,' Harry muttered. 'Right through the nose.'

'I overheard the address. That woman Sue's voice is like a fog horn,' said Nick, but nobody was listening to him.

'It's not really his fault.'
'No?'
'I mean – it was those louts who broke it down.'
'And they wouldn't have been here if Frank hadn't been here.' Harry paused in his deadly logic. 'And Frank wouldn't have been here if Ken hadn't allowed him to be here. And I wouldn't have been held at knife-point if Frank hadn't been here. So it's all Ken's fault.' He paused for breath. 'Yes?'
'No.'
'How do you see it then?'
'I know where they've gone,' said Nick. But still no one listened.
'I see it this way – it wasn't Ken's fault.'
'Yeah.'
'I mean it was you who dreamed up Box Thirteen. What do you expect? And now we don't know where he's gone or what kind of trouble he's in.'
'I don't *care* what kind of trouble he's in. What about my bleeding door?'
'I know where they've gone,' said Nick, but by that time they were too annoyed with each other to notice him.
'Okay, you've had your problems, Harry. But you've got your health and strength. You left the brigade of your own choice.'
'With one arm twisted behind me back,' he said bitterly.
'But you weren't chucked out.'
'Neither was he.'
'It felt like it. And you haven't got dodgy lungs. All you're worrying about is a door. For all we know, Ken could be lying under a bus, or being mauled by those apes.'
Harry had the grace to look chastened. There was an uneasy silence, unexpectedly broken by Nick.
'I know where they've gone,' he said patiently.

'What?' Doreen and Harry spoke in unison as they rounded on him. 'Why didn't you tell us before?'

'You're exceeding the limit.' The policeman was grey-faced.

'Yeah – I have to get somewhere fast.'

'Yes?'

'To stop a domestic dispute from turning into a riot. Can you give me an escort?'

'I beg your pardon?'

Already Ken was beginning to regret his plan, to realise how naïve it all was. 'Er – I'm going to a domestic—'

'Whose?'

'A friend.'

'And—'

'I wonder if you'd escort me.' He glanced down at his watch in angry frustration.

'I'm afraid we can't get involved in domestic disputes,' said the policeman. He was young, a going-by-the-book man. His eyes were ice-chip blue and a little chilly smile played at the corners of his mouth. 'And you're exceeding the speed limit.'

'I know. I—'

'So I shall have to book you.'

Ken's heart sank. 'Look – don't you think there are mitigating—'

'Circumstances for your speeding? No, sir, there aren't any.'

'What about a bloke driving a pregnant woman to hospital?'

'Are you a pregnant woman?' He was writing out a slip of paper. 'Can I see your papers, sir?'

'They're at home.'

'Will you produce them at your nearest police station within seven days?'

'Okay.'

'Now, if you'd care to dismount.'

'Look – I'm in a tearing hurry.'

'If you could dismount, sir, I'd like to have a look at the bike.'

'Watch it.'

McGeary's Cortina shrieked to a halt at the junction, just too late to avoid clipping the wing of an ice-cream van. It slewed round in the road and went up a grass verge where it came to rest.

'You lot stay here,' said McGeary, hurrying out of the car. 'I'll sort it out. Doesn't look as if there's much damage done.'

He strode purposefully over the road to the van which bore the title of Mr Whipsy painted on its side. It was true that there was little damage but the driver didn't seem convinced. He was a very tall, very broad man who seemed to have been poured into the driver's seat.

'You bloody idiot!' he said, extricating himself from the van. 'You came across that drive like a bat out of hell! It wasn't your right of way.'

'Okay. It was my chauffeur's fault actually. I don't think there's a lot of damage been done.'

'I'll see about that,' said the ice-cream man, beginning to pace round the van, pointing out a selection of dents and scratches including a huge dent on the side which McGeary's Cortina had not touched. The ice-cream man was built like a house but McGeary was not going to pay for the large dented area he hadn't dented.

'Look,' said McGeary, 'we didn't do that.'

'And I says you did – and you're going to pay.' He strode towards the Cortina.

The policeman was making more than heavy weather of White Lightning. He had checked the tyres, the exhaust and was now beginning a detailed investigation of the engine.

'Look here,' said Ken again. 'I'm pushed.'

'It looks as if this bike's been pushed too, doesn't it?' he said, staring down at the machine gloomily.

At that moment another police car rolled up. Not more trouble, thought Ken miserably. A figure emerged – a familiar one.

'Ken?'

'Andy Shaw!' Suddenly Ken knew that everything was going to be all right. At least for the moment.

The young policeman looked up annoyed. 'Sergeant—'

'Afternoon Blackwood. Having a spot of bother with this young villain here?'

Ken grinned hopefully.

'He was speeding in a built-up area, sir. And now I'm giving his bike the once over. He said he wanted an escort,' said Blackwood with withering sarcasm. 'I don't know who the hell he thinks he is.'

'I do. Mr Boon is well known to me.' And, as if quoting from a citation for distinguished conduct, he continued: 'He was forced to resign from the fire brigade, where he'd been a serving officer for some eighteen years, because of damaged lungs received in the course of the rescue of a family. He's a hero. You will escort Mr Boon to wherever he has to go. And you will be on discreet stand-by, Blackwood, to ensure that law and order is upheld.'

'Yes, sir.'

Sergeant Shaw turned to Ken and shook his hand. 'How's life treating you?'

'Okay, Andy. Odd jobs, you know.'

'You'd best be off then – and Ken—'

'Yeah?'

'Keep PC Blackwood in sight,' he whispered.

* * *

'How much do you want?' sighed McGeary as the Cortina rocked violently from side to side. 'Not a complete re-spray, I trust. But I'd like to make good the damage we caused.'

The ice-cream man stopped rocking the car and shrugged. 'A ton might cover it.'

'Can't do it . . .' The ice-cream man tightened his grip on the Cortina. 'But I'll give you what I've got on me,' continued McGeary. 'Say, half a ton.'

'Sixty.'

'Fifty-five.'

He began to rock the car again. 'Sixty.'

'Okay.' McGeary passed him the notes and the ice-cream man counted them. Then he walked back towards the van, grinning. 'When you run your own business, mister, you gotta look after it.'

'Sure,' said McGeary bitterly.

'Thanks,' said Ken to an infuriated PC Blackwood a few streets away from the Brandons. 'I'll carry on alone now.'

'Of course – any time you'd like an escort service,' he replied sarcastically, 'just give me a ring.'

'I will,' said Ken and drove on, leaving Blackwood parked by the roadside. 'I'll give you a shout if anyone breaks the law,' he shouted over his shoulder.

Blackwood gritted his teeth.

Pat was hurtling the Cortina along now at 60 mph, and as he rushed a red light a couple of streets away from the Brandons, they all heard the wail of a police siren. Flagged down, they waited until PC Blackwood slowly strode towards them.

'Good afternoon.' He smiled icily.

'Terribly sorry, officer,' said McGeary. 'We're on the way to a bothersome situation.'

'Are you now?' His voice became even more icy. 'I wonder – are you going to ask me for a police escort?'

'No,' said McGeary. 'Definitely not.' He tried to ease the edge off his tone. 'Although it's most kind of you to—'

'I didn't offer,' said PC Blackwood. 'I definitely didn't offer. And now, might I see your insurance and your driving licence?'

'I'm afraid in both cases—'

'Seven days. At your police station. And now, for speeding in a built-up area . . .' He began to write slowly.

The Brandon house looked as neglected as ever. In fact there was such a desolate atmosphere that Ken felt a shiver shooting up his spine. Removal men were loading a large sofa on to the truck and they were just about to close the tailboard. Harry's mini was half up the kerb, but apart from that there was an unexpected atmosphere of torpor.

Ken shut off White Lightning and dismounted. He hurried over to the mini and stared inside. The driver's door was open and the key was still in the ignition. Ken hesitated, then took the keys and slammed the door. 'Any sign of the driver?' he said to one of the removal men.

'Search me. Funny bloke inside though. In fact there's a bit of a scene going on. Shouldn't be surprised if it ends in tears before bedtime.'

Ken ran up the weed-strewn garden path and in through the front door. As he walked into the living-room he saw the familiar shape of a raised shovel.

It was an ugly little scene. Mrs Brandon was standing beside her terrified husband with her trusty shovel raised on high. Frank was threatening Brandon with his fists and Ken was relieved to see that there was no sign of the knife. Frank didn't seem to have noticed the shovel, or perhaps he just didn't believe in it.

'Leave my husband alone. You're mad,' Mrs Brandon was saying, her voice soaring up the scale.

Certainly Frank looked quite deranged, with his bulging eyes and contorted features. As for Brandon, he kept saying 'Let's talk this one over, old boy' in a very high voice. Frank tried to push Mrs Brandon aside and she waved the shovel ineffectually.

Would she ever use it? Ken wondered. 'Take it easy, Frank,' he said from the doorway and all three of them swung round.

'You again!' said Mrs Brandon.

'You! – Brian,' said Brandon wildly.

'Stay out of this Ken. This is none of your business,' said Frank sternly.

But Ken wasn't having any. 'Come on, Frank. Leave it alone.'

But Frank was adamant. 'I'm a man betrayed, Ken. Here's me busting a gut on those bloody rigs, earning the greenies, while this Brandon is between my sheets.' He turned back to the object of his hatred. 'You're dead.'

'Now look, old boy, let's talk this one over,' gabbled Brandon repetitively.

'Is that true?' asked Mrs Brandon of Ken.

'Is what true?' Ken suddenly felt exhausted. If this was the life of a private eye they could stick it.

Frustrated, she turned back to her husband. 'Is it true . . . about his wife? Did you sleep with her?'

'The man's mad.'

'Is he?' She stared at her husband for a minute. 'Peter, I don't believe you.'

'She doesn't believe you,' said Frank, dancing from one foot to the other. Ken noticed that his enforced rest seemed to have made him very active.

'My dear, I assure you, this chap is completely potty.'

Mrs Brandon stared at her husband penetratingly and then came to a determined conclusion. She raised the shovel high above her head and her husband reeled back. At last, thought Ken. She really is going to use it.

But Frank didn't want competition. 'I'm first,' he shouted as he made a dive for Brandon. He didn't get any further because Ken grabbed him. While they struggled the spade rose higher and higher. Then there was a bull-like cry from the hall – McGeary, Sue, Pat and Gerry had arrived. They all strode in, looking as if they had just made a journey over the Alps.

Doreen drove slowly past the parked police car.

'Wonder if he's anticipating trouble?' said Harry.

'Mm – if it hasn't started already.'

'Don't worry. Ken will calm things down. He's a good peacemaker.'

'Yes,' said Doreen. 'He sounds it after what happened at McGeary's!'

'He was provoked.'

'You're a strange man, Harry.'

'Thanks.'

'Okay. But one moment you're against him, next moment you're for him. Mercurial.'

'What?'

'Mood swings.'

Harry laughed. 'That's how everyone reacts to Ken. You try it.'

'No thanks.'

'I thought you were mates.'

'We are – but that's all.' Now she was out of the police car's sight she began to accelerate. 'Let's get on with it, shall we?' she snapped.

But Harry only smiled.

'Right, Francis, you and me have got some business to attend to,' said McGeary, standing on the threshold like some demonic version of a 'This is Your Life' host.

'Sue!' said Brandon. 'Oh Christ!'

'Sue? Is this her?' asked Mrs Brandon.

'Sue!' said Frank.

Sue was more fulsome. 'Don't hurt him, Tom. Please don't hurt him. I love him.'

It was a touching picture as they all stared at her open-mouthed with the widest possible range of emotions.

'You can still love him after I've finished with him,' said McGeary unsympathetically. He turned slowly to Brandon.

'He's for it and all. Brandon, you're at the bottom of this trouble, mate, and you're next on the list.'

'Now just hang on, old boy. Can't we—'

'Don't you touch Peter!' Mrs Brandon ceremoniously raised her shovel in another direction. No, thought Ken, she's never going to use it – she never does use it.

'Get them both,' said McGeary with authority and both his lieutenants lumbered forward at the pace of apathetic snails.

Mrs Brandon waved her shovel at them. 'Get off my property, you morons! Get out! Leave my husband alone.' She had come full circle in a surprising volte-face and Ken noted with some amusement that now her husband was under attack she was completely partisan.

'Get on with it,' yelled McGeary to Pat and Gerry, but they seemed strangely subdued. Clearly they were not making sufficient progress for their irate boss and he began to yell at them all over again.

Ken, fascinated by their inertia and Mrs Brandon's shovel symbolism, decided to see how the deadlock developed without interfering. Then he had an idea.

'Oi,' he whispered at Frank and Sue, who were watching, transfixed by the ebb and flow of the near deadlock.

'What do you want?' hissed Frank.

'Get away now – get down the garden path.'

'No. I'm going to fix Brandon if it's the last thing I do.'

'It may well be.'

'I'm not afraid of his henchmen.'

'Look, there's gonna be trouble. Don't you want Sue out of this?'

'Sue?'

'Your wife. Make it up to her. Get her out of here.'

Frank thought carefully. 'Okay, Ken,' he said at last. 'We'll do a bunk. And thanks for everything.' They took the hint and shot down the garden path whilst Mrs Brandon, using her shovel like a lance, kept Pat and Gerry at bay.

Gerry lunged close to Brandon. 'Get off him!' she shrieked and struck out. Gerry dodged but McGeary got in the way.

'Look out!' yelled Ken. Much to his amazement, Mrs Brandon had used the weapon at last – but only by mistake. Hit by the flat of the spade, McGeary went down like a ton of bricks. Everybody stopped and stared down at the flattened ox of a man.

'Oh God!' wailed Mrs Brandon appalled. 'Did I do that?'

There was a long, thoughtful pause. 'I think you did,' said Ken at last.

'Oh no,' said Brandon whilst Ken bent over McGeary. 'Whatever have you done?'

'Is he dead?' said Pat with interest.

McGeary began to groan.

'Not quite,' said Ken drily as Harry and Doreen came rushing in.

'Everything all right?' asked Harry. 'Sorry we're late.'

'Well – as good as can be expected.'

'And your client?' asked Doreen.

'I believe he's making good his escape.'

'Where am I?' moaned McGeary. 'What's happened?'

'Not another memory lapse, I hope,' said Ken.

'No,' said McGeary. 'I remember everything. Every bloody thing.' He closed his eyes.

The removal van lurched down the road, the driver only too anxious to put as much space between him and the domestic conflict at the Brandon house as possible. On the sofa by the door sat Frank and Sue. For a mile or so they remained unreconciled, incommunicado. They stared out at the never-changing suburban scene, intent only on their own thoughts.

'I'm sorry,' said Frank suddenly, breaking the silence.

There was a longish pause.

'So am I,' said Sue.

'I missed you.'

'Did you?' she asked doubtfully.

'As soon as I remembered you, I missed you,' qualified Frank.

Sue laughed. 'I'm glad we got away,' she said. 'That could've turned nasty.'

'Yeah,' said Frank. 'Ken persuaded me. But I'm still sorry I didn't sort out Brandon.'

'You sorted me out instead.'

'I said I'm sorry.'

'Yes,' she took his hand. 'I didn't mean to bring it up again.'

He kissed one of her black eyes. 'I love you,' he said.

The removal van gave an extra large lurch, sending them sprawling into each other. Luckily the sofa saved them from any bruises. 'Handy,' said Sue, smiling.

'Very.' Frank kissed her again and then a sudden, unpleasant thought crept into his mind. 'Hey, this is Brandon's sofa! Did you . . .?'

'No,' she said quickly. 'Honest, Frank, we didn't.'

'Because if you did I'm going after him again. If you think I'm sitting here when—'

'I *said* we didn't.'

'Okay. I think it'd be better if I forgot all about this business.' He kissed her again but she broke away, alarmed.

'I don't want you to forget anything, love. Never, never again.'

The van turned a sudden corner and once more they collapsed in a heap.

'I won't forget,' said Frank. 'Not now. How could I?'

'If I were you I'd have him along to casualty,' said Harry. There was no compassion in his voice and he gazed down at McGeary without interest.

'Yeah,' said Pat without any conviction.

Ken stood outside with Doreen and the Brandons looking on as McGeary's two lieutenants heaved up their grunting and groaning boss between them and trundled him down the path. There seemed little for him to do at this stage and he felt a wave of inertia sweep over him. A thought occurred to him.

'If I were you,' he said to Brandon, 'I'd get on with your move.'

'We will, darling, won't we?' He gave his wife a nervous smile. 'Shall we follow up the removal van? Might as well get going.'

But Mrs Brandon clearly had no intention of

complying with anything he wanted. Ever again. She turned quickly and began to walk purposefully back into the house. Brandon followed her lamely, calling endearments and being ignored.

'Just don't leave a forwarding address,' Ken advised him.

Ken and Doreen walked over to Harry as McGeary was driven off. 'Okay?' said Ken, handing him his car keys.

'What do you mean, okay? Have you seen the door of number five? It's ruined.'

Ken looked a little sheepish. 'I really am sorry about that. I should've been quicker off the mark with the other key.'

But Harry was grinning at him in the old, taunting way.

Doreen handed Ken his helmet. 'You'll need this to get home. You forgot to take it,' she reproved.

'I was in a rush.'

'Well, like they say, fools rush in . . . but I s'pose private eyes have to take risks.'

She walked away, back to her car, whilst Harry got into his mini-van.

'Let's get back. Nick's in charge – and that's always dodgy.'

'Harry.'

'Yes?'

'I'm sorry about the door.'

Harry grinned. 'Forget it – all in a day's work.'

'Mine maybe, but not yours.'

'Oh I don't know,' said Harry with a wink. 'It's an exciting life – being associated with a private eye.'

'I don't know about that.'

'Well, it's "anything legal considered", isn't it?'

'Sometimes it is.'

Harry switched on the engine. 'I'm looking forward to an exciting old age,' he said and drove away.

Thoughtfully Ken put his helmet on and tried to start the bike. Nothing happened. Ken tried again. Still nothing. Harry's car was rounding the bend now and there was no chance of alerting him. Then Doreen drove past. She hooted, but Ken reacted too late to flag her down. Her car disappeared in the opposite direction to Harry, and Ken was left standing by his bike. Gloomily he tried again – but there was not even a whimper of life.

Ken sat down on the kerb and contemplated his future. Part of his assets reposed by the kerb – an ancient and broken down bike. That, a field, a caravan that was originally a site office, a few bits and pieces, these were all he had in the world. His determination about the market garden remained but *en route* to its opening he would have to make some kind of living. So, without doubt, it would be anything legal considered.